"The castle [   ] aree hundred sixty-five [   ]

Alice said, " [   ] of them."

"I am afraid [   ] time," the *Duc* said. "But I promise that you will see not only the best of Chaumont, but parts that are not open to the public, and for which only I have the key."

"Oh thank you . . . thank you!" Alice cried. "Can we start now?"

Lencia spoke before the *Duc* could answer. "No, of course not! *Monsieur le Duc* wishes to return to his own Chateau."

Alice knew it was a rebuke. "I am very sorry," she said. "It is all so exciting, and even more exciting now that we have met you, because now we shall not have to trail around with a group of sightseers, and you promised I shall see the secret places where no-one else is allowed! Oh! I am so glad we came!"

"So am I," the *Duc* said. He was answering Alice . . . but he was looking at Lencia . . .

A Camfield Novel of Love by Barbara Cartland

"Barbara Cartland's novels are all distinguished by their intelligence, good sense, and good nature. . . ."
— **ROMANTIC TIMES**

"Who could give better advice on how to keep your romance going strong than the world's most famous romance novelist, Barbara Cartland?"
— **THE STAR**

Camfield Place,
Hatfield,
Hertfordshire,
England

Dearest Reader,

Camfield Novels of Love mark a very exciting era of my books with Jove. They have already published nearly two hundred of my titles since they became my first publisher in America, and now all my original paperback romances in the future will be published exclusively by them.

As you already know, Camfield Place in Hertford-shire is my home, which originally existed in 1275, but was rebuilt in 1867 by the grandfather of Beatrix Potter.

It was here in this lovely house, with the best view in the county, that she wrote *The Tale of Peter Rabbit*. Mr. McGregor's garden is exactly as she described it. The door in the wall that the fat little rabbit could not squeeze underneath and the goldfish pool where the white cat sat twitching its tail are still there.

I had Camfield Place blessed when I came here in 1950 and was so happy with my husband until he died, and now with my children and grandchildren, that I know the atmosphere is filled with love and we have all been very lucky.

It is easy here to write of love and I know you will enjoy the Camfield Novels of Love. Their plots are definitely exciting and the covers very romantic. They come to you, like all my books, with love.

Bless you,

CAMFIELD NOVELS OF LOVE
by Barbara Cartland

A NEW CAMFIELD NOVEL OF LOVE BY

Barbara Cartland

A Magical Moment

JOVE BOOKS, NEW YORK

A MAGICAL MOMENT

A Jove Book / published by arrangement with
the author

PRINTING HISTORY
Jove edition / April 1995

ISBN: 0-515-11594-0

A JOVE BOOK®
Jove Books are published by The Berkley Publishing Group,
200 Madison Avenue, New York, New York 10016.
JOVE and the "J" design are trademarks
belonging to Jove Publications, Inc.

PRINTED IN THE UNITED STATES OF AMERICA

10 9 8 7 6 5 4 3 2 1

Author's Note

WHEN I visited the Castles of the Loire Valley in 1990 I had forgotten that Chaumont was the perfect fairy-tale Castle.

In the sunshine, it looked as if it might disappear at any moment.

Because it was spared by the Revolution, it is without exception the most exquisite Castle in France.

One can well believe that the work which began in 1519 by King François I was said by his rival, Charles the Fifth, the Holy Roman Emperor to be, "a summary of all that human industry can achieve."

Some of the rooms like the King's Bedroom which are furnished and unchanged make it all the more thrilling.

The successors after François' death showed little interest in the Castle, preferring their Royal Palace in Paris.

Louis XIII made several trips to Chaumont before leaving the Castle and the county to his brother Gaston d'Orléans.

The Prince, we are told, enjoyed showing his daughter, the future Grande Mademoiselle, the tricks of the famous grand staircase whose double spirals enabled two people to go up and down at the same time without ever crossing each other's paths.

There are so many Castles to see in the Loire Valley that it is impossible to mention them all.

Chaumont gave me this story, and some years ago another Castle built on the edge of the dark, mysterious forest of Chinon in the Indre Valley gave me another.

I was inspired to write "The Castle Made for Love" about it, just as Perrault was inspired to write "The Tale of the Sleeping Beauty."

The Castles of Usse and Chaumont are the two most beautiful fairy-tale buildings I have ever seen.

I am sure the other Castles one by one will become centres of romance as the years go by.

We look more eagerly than we have ever done before for the real love which seems for the moment lost in the obsession of the media with sex.

This is not the romance for which men have fought and died over the centuries.

A Magical Moment

chapter one

1895

"OH, no, Papa, you cannot mean it!" Lady Lencia Leigh exclaimed.

"You promised, you promised!" her younger sister Alice cried. "How can you change now at the very last minute?"

"I am very sorry, girls," the Earl of Armeron replied, "but your Stepmother has set her heart on going to Sweden, and a Prince does not celebrate his seventieth birthday very often."

He tried to make it a joke, but both his daughters were looking at him reproachfully.

They were thinking that ever since he had married for the second time, the Earl had changed.

He was no longer the fond, loving Father he had been before, and was now someone who seemed to them almost a stranger.

When the Earl's wife had died a year ago, he had sunk into the depths of despair from which, it seemed, no-one could arouse him.

It was his friend the Marquis of Salisbury who had suggested that he should go with him for a holiday to the South of France.

The Marquis had recently built himself a very large and impressive villa near Nice.

He said to the Earl he wanted his expert advice in planning the garden.

Looking back at what had occurred, his daughters realised it had been the first step towards a tragedy.

They had never for one moment imagined their Father would marry again.

He had adored their Mother as they all had, and the whole family had been very close and extremely happy together.

It had always been a disappointment to the Earl that he had no son and therefore no direct heir to inherit the title.

But he had been extremely proud of his eldest daughter, Lencia.

She closely resembled her Mother, who had been an outstanding beauty.

So great was the resemblance that at first, after his wife's death, the Earl had been almost reluctant to look at Lencia.

She had the same fair hair, the same sparkling blue eyes, and the same exquisite pink and white complexion.

But Lencia also had a kind of spiritual aura about her which made her different from all other girls of her age.

She was also very intelligent.

That was not surprising, considering how clever her Father was.

Besides this, she had a marked personality of her own, which unfortunately her Stepmother, the new Countess, had noticed the moment she stepped into Armeron Castle.

The Earl had been away from home for six weeks and they were excitedly awaiting his return.

Lencia had received a letter from him the day before he was due to arrive.

"A letter from Papa!" she exclaimed when the Butler brought it to her.

"I hope he has not changed his mind at the last moment," Alice said, "and intends to stay on longer in the South of France."

"Papa must realise there is a lot to do here," Lencia assured her.

She opened the envelope as she spoke.

Taking out her Father's letter, she read a little of it before she exclaimed.

"It cannot be true!"

"What has happened?" Alice asked.

Lencia looked at the letter again before she said in a voice which did not sound like her own:

"Papa has . . . married again!"

"I do not believe it!" Alice declared.

But it was true, and when the new Countess arrived, everything was changed.

The girls had waited for her apprehensively.

When their Father appeared with his new wife clinging to his arm, it was impossible for either of them to run towards him eagerly as they had always done before.

Madame Flaubert was characteristic of the exotic, chic French woman.

She might almost have stepped straight out of a novelette.

She was not beautiful, but good-looking, and made the very most of her looks.

She was amusing and witty, and almost every word she spoke seemed to have a *double entendre.*

She flattered the Earl not only in words but with her eyes, her mouth, and her hands.

Lencia realised her Father was fascinated by her because she was so very different from the wife he had lost.

Madame Flaubert had gone to Nice looking for a man to escort her.

The meeting with the Earl was a dream come true.

She had always hoped to marry again.

But the Frenchmen who paid her compliments and laughed at everything she said did not offer her marriage.

She saw the Earl, morose and depressed, but at the same time still a very handsome man.

A rich Englishman with a title!

She felt the gates of opportunity opening in front of her.

She had never worked so hard at presenting herself as she did after meeting the Earl.

By shameless wheedling she got herself invited by the Marquis to stay in his Villa.

Her sob-story was that she had been unable to get into the Hotel where she always stayed.

That the noise in the Hotel she had been forced to go to was intolerable and the discomfort indescribable would have appealled to any kind man's heart.

The Marquis was in fact finding the Earl somewhat heavy on the hand.

Therefore he invited Madame Flaubert and another friend he had known for years to move from where they were staying into the Villa.

From that moment, although he was not aware of it, there was for the Earl no escape.

Madame Flaubert paid him compliments until he smiled.

She set herself out to amuse him until he laughed.

He could not help feeling flattered when she told him how much she loved him.

He was, in fact, not quite certain how he found himself being married officially at the *Mairie*.

As their religions were different, they dispensed with a marriage service to follow in a Church.

They were nevertheless legally married.

Madame Flaubert had a new gold wedding-ring on her left hand to prove it.

The Earl was not the only person who had told her of the beauty and importance of Armeron Castle.

The Marquis, who had stayed there often, described it as one of the finest examples of Medieval building in the country.

The gardens, which had been created by the last Earl, were to his mind, he said, finer than any other garden he had ever seen.

The congratulations the new Countess of Armeron had received did not however prepare her for the first sight of her elder stepdaughter.

She had expected that both the girls would be pretty.

"How could they be anything else?" she asked the Earl. "When you, Dearest, are so handsome that I know every woman's heart turns over when she looks at you."

"You flatter me," the Earl said, but he was quite prepared to listen to more.

The new wife, however, had a severe shock when she walked into the Drawing-Room where Lencia and Alice were waiting.

They felt shy and, although they tried not to admit it, somewhat hostile towards their Stepmother.

They were not waiting for them in the hall, where the Earl had expected to find them.

Instead, they were standing in the beautiful room which had always seemed the perfect background for their Mother.

The blue curtains and coverings on the chairs and sofas had echoed her eyes, while the glittering crystal chandeliers had the same sparkle which shone in her eyes whenever she saw someone she loved.

The Earl would have walked into the room first.

But his wife put her arm in his so that they came in side by side.

Just for a moment there was complete silence.

"Here we are, girls," the Earl said, "and I have been so looking forward to seeing you."

With an effort Lencia moved forward.

It was then her Stepmother drew in her breath.

This was certainly a rival she had not expected—a girl very young and so lovely that it was impossible even for a woman not to stare at her and go on staring.

Lencia kissed her Father and he kissed her back.

"We have been longing to have you back, Papa," she said.

As she spoke, she could not help looking with some surprise at the woman holding tightly to his arm.

The Countess had dressed herself to impress.

She was wearing a hat trimmed with ostrich feathers.

Their colour was echoed by the ruby ear-rings that dangled from her ears.

There was a ruby brooch pinned to the shoulder of her black satin cape.

She was certainly elegant, but at the same time there was something theatrical about her.

Lencia knew instinctively she was incongruous in her Mother's Drawing-Room, or indeed in the Castle itself.

"Now you must meet my daughters," the Earl was saying.

"Yvonne, this is Lencia, who, as I told you, should have been presented in Court last year, but will instead curtsy to the Queen next month."

Neither of the women spoke, and the Earl went on quickly:

"This is Alice, who is just seventeen, but I expect she will want to join in some of the festivities to which her sister is invited."

"They are much older than I had expected," the Countess said. "I thought, Dearest, seeing how young you look, your daughters would still be in the nursery."

This was obviously the sort of flattery the Earl had listened to and found so enjoyable in Nice.

Somehow it seemed more than a little out of place at this particular moment.

"I am sure, Papa," Lencia said, "that you are longing for your tea. It is all ready for you."

She moved towards the fireplace as she spoke.

The Earl and his new wife followed her.

The tea was laid out as it always had been in front of the sofa.

There was the traditional shining silver teapot and kettle.

Also the Queen Anne tea-caddy in which the very first tea from Ceylon had been served in the Castle.

There was also an imposing display of warm scones,

cucumber sandwiches, fruit-cakes, iced-cakes, and several other dainties for which the Armeron kitchens were famous.

As they reached the table with its long lace-edged cloth, Lencia said to the Countess:

"Will you pour it or would you like me to do so?"

It was a question that the Countess recognised immediately as significant.

With hardly a pause she replied:

"Of course I will do it. I know exactly how your dear, handsome Father likes his tea."

She swept with a rustle of silk petticoats and a whiff of exotic perfume to sit in the centre of the sofa, facing the silver tray.

It was where their Mother had always sat, and it was at that moment Lencia knew how much she resented the intruder, a woman who she was certain would never take her Mother's place in the Castle or anywhere else.

At the same time, as the afternoon and evening passed, she had to admit that her Father was in better spirits than when he had gone away.

He was certainly finding his new wife most amusing.

Only when they had gone upstairs to go to bed did Alice say in a whisper:

"How could he have brought anyone like that to take Mama's place?"

"She makes him laugh," Lencia had answered. "But . . ."

She bit back the words she was going to say.

What was the point of fighting against the inevitable?

Their Father, whom they loved and who had been so very much a part of their lives, had somehow left them.

"We have lost not only our Mother but also our Father,"

Lencia said to herself bitterly as she got into bed.

In the days that followed she was to think the same again and again.

The new Countess was determined not to be ignored.

She intended to assert herself in what she thought was her rightful position from the moment she arrived.

She gave orders to the servants in a sharp voice, but to the Earl she was all honey and sweetness.

She flattered him not only in words but by seeming to watch over and tend him.

She would fetch his cigar-case almost before he wanted it.

She would pat the cushion before he sat down in the chair.

She was at his side almost every moment of the day.

There was no doubt, Lencia had to admit to herself, that he seemed younger in years.

Yet she felt embarrassed at the blatant manner in which her Stepmother flattered her Father and flirted with him quite openly regardless of who was there.

Alice watched them wide-eyed, as if it was a performance and she was the audience.

Because to Lencia her Stepmother's behaviour seemed so vulgar, whenever she could she kept away from her Father and his new wife.

The girls had planned with their Father, before he went to Nice, that he would take them to France before the Season in London started.

Alice had been reading about the Castles of the Loire Valley.

The Earl knew them well and had promised to take the girls to see Chaumont, which was the largest and the most impressive of all the Castles in that part of France.

They had both been looking forward to it wildly.

To Alice it was particularly exciting because she had just grown old enough to read some of the great love stories of the world.

One which had captured her imagination more than any other had been the story of the famous Beauty Diane de Poitiers.

She was loved to distraction by Henry II of France even though she was eighteen years older than he was.

Alice was determined to see where Diane's monogram was carved on the parapet wall of Chaumont she had restored.

"It is the letter 'D,' " she said excitedly, "surrounded by attributes of the goddess after whom she was named."

"You shall see it all, my Dearest," the Earl had said, "and I promise you will not be disappointed. I have seen a great many French Castles and *Châteaux*, but of them all I think Chaumont is the most exciting and certainly the most impressive."

He sighed.

"I wish I could have stayed there when King François and I enjoyed the marvellous hunting available in what was then a deserted area."

The girls were listening intently, and he went on:

"He had the old hunting-lodge razed to the ground and began the construction of this sumptuous Palace, which will thrill you as it thrilled me when I first saw it as a boy."

It was the first time her Father had seemed enthusiastic about anything since her Mother's death.

They had therefore made him plan the date they should go and how long they should stay.

"We must see heaps of other Castles too while we are there," Alice said eagerly.

"I can see I shall have to read up my history," her Father said, "but we will certainly see all we can. I shall expect you both to speak perfect French by the time we return."

"We will try, Papa, we really will try," Alice promised.

As Lencia knew she would, for the next month Alice talked of very little except their visit to France.

She sought out in the extensive Library at Armeron all the books which mentioned the Loire Valley.

She put them ready to be packed with their luggage when they set off to Chaumont on what to her was a pilgrimage.

Now two weeks after the Earl had returned home he was telling them that the visit would have to be postponed.

"We will go another time," he said, "I promise you."

But Alice protested volubly.

"You know, Papa, that once we go to London and Lencia is presented, there will be too many other engagements for us to get away. There will be Ascot and finally Goodwood, where you will be running your horses."

Her voice rose as she cried:

"Oh, Papa, how can you fail us now, when everything was fixed?"

"I am sorry, my Dear," the Earl said, "but I promise you I will find another time when it is possible for me to leave England."

The way he spoke told Lencia only too clearly that it was unlikely their Stepmother would be willing to leave London during the Season.

She was also convinced that she would not allow her husband to go off with his two daughters without her.

"That reminds me," the Earl said unexpectedly. "I am

afraid, Lencia, my Dearest, we will have to change the Drawing-Room at which you are presented."

Lencia stared at him.

"Why, Papa?"

"Because, my Dearest, I am sure you will understand that I must first present your Stepmother on our marriage. She thinks it would be a mistake for you to be presented at the same time."

Lencia drew in her breath.

It had been planned that she should be presented last year, just before she was eighteen.

Then, when the Countess died, they had been in deep mourning.

The presentation obviously had to be postponed until the first Drawing-Room the following year, which would take place at the beginning of May.

Her Father had gone to see the Lord Chamberlain and everything was arranged.

He was opening Armeron House in Park Lane.

Because her Mother could not present Lencia, the Earl's elder sister, who was a Lady of the Bedchamber, had volunteered to do so.

It had never occurred to Lencia for one moment that having missed her presentation last May, she would be asked to postpone it a second time.

She knew the procedure on those occasions quite well and said:

"But if you, Papa, can present Stepmama, why in her turn, as I know has been done before, can she not present me?"

There was a short silence before the Earl answered:

"I did suggest that, but your Stepmother says, my Dear, that it makes her feel old, when she is still so young, to be chaperoning a girl of your age."

Lencia knew quite well that was not the reason.

What her Stepmother was afraid of was that she would outshine her.

Because Lencia was very unselfconscious, she thought this idea was absurd, yet because she was a woman she understood.

In fact, the new Countess had been very evasive about her age.

She and Alice had soon realised it was not a subject that should be discussed.

"Very well, Papa," Lencia said, "if it must be changed, then it must."

"I am sure there will be no difficulties," the Earl said. "The Lord Chamberlain will understand, and there will be several more Drawing-Rooms, the last I believe being in June."

"Supposing they are all full up?" Alice asked unexpectedly.

"I cannot believe that I shall be refused a place for my daughter," the Earl said.

He spoke in a manner which his children jokingly called his "Armeron Air."

It was something that happened only occasionally because the Earl was in fact a friendly and easy-going man.

But if his pride was hurt or he was insulted in any way, then his family background, which was a very distinguished one, would come to the surface.

His Armeron voice would pulverise the person who had offended him.

"It would be dreadful," Alice said, "if poor Lencia has to miss being presented at Court, just as I am very sorry for myself in not being able to see Chaumont."

"You will see it, of course you will see it," the Earl

said. "It is just that your Stepmother has set her heart on going to Sweden, and it would be very unkind of me if I refused her."

"I expect really she wants to wear the Armeron Tiara and associate with all those Princes and Princesses," Alice said. "I do not suppose she knew people like that before she married you, Papa."

It was only Alice, Lencia thought, who would put thoughts like that into words.

Because it was something that was undeniably true, the Earl had looked at the clock on the mantelpiece and said:

"It is time we were all getting dressed for dinner. You know I dislike having to wait for my meals."

He walked out of the room as he spoke and the two girls were left alone.

"It is not fair!" Alice raged. "Our Stepmother is determined that he should not go away with us. When I was talking about the beauty of the Castles, she said, 'They are not really very interesting, most of them are empty.' Fancy her feeling like that!"

Alice's voice was scathing.

Lencia knew quite well that their Stepmother, as the Countess of Armeron, wanted to share in the social world of London.

She was not the least interested in anything that had happened in the past.

"It is no use, Alice," Lencia said. "If we cannot go, then we cannot go. We shall just have to stay here and wait for them to come back."

"When they do, I bet she will find some way to prevent you and me going to London with her and Papa," Alice complained.

She thought for a moment, then went on:

"She wants him to herself and to give big Dinner Parties at Armeron House. She will say I am too young to attend them and that *débutantes* and their parties are a bore."

"Oh, Alice, you cannot be sure she will say that," Lencia protested.

"She will, because I have heard her say it already," Alice asserted. "She was talking to that lady's-maid of hers when I passed the door. They were speaking in French, thinking no-one would understand. But I heard Stepmama say: '*Débutantes* are a bore, and the people I want to meet are to be found in London. So the sooner we get there, the better.'"

Lencia knew quite well what her Stepmother was talking about.

There had already been controversy about the Ball her Father would give for her which had been postponed from the previous year.

The discussion, when her Mother was still alive, was whether they should have the Ball in London or in the Country.

It had finally been decided that it would be nice for Lencia to meet girls of her own age.

They would give a large Ball in London, and later several smaller dances in the Country.

Now Lencia guessed those plans were to be put on one side.

Of course her Stepmother was bored with *débutantes*.

She could understand that.

At the same time, she felt that she and Alice were being pushed aside by a strong and determined hand.

Soon they would find themselves moving out of their Father's life.

"I am exaggerating everything, of course I am," Lencia told herself severely.

At the same time, she was honest enough to know that her Stepmother disliked her and found both her and Alice an encumbrance.

She was continually talking of the things they would do in London when her Father opened the house, as he intended to do at the end of the month.

It was most unfortunate, Lencia thought, that two or three days ago the Swedish Ambassador had called at Armeron.

A neighbour with whom he was staying had brought him to see the Castle because it was an outstanding architectural feature of the County and a notable beauty-spot.

The new Countess had made a great fuss over the Ambassador.

In fact, when they were walking in the garden, Lencia could now remember that she took him on one side.

Ostensibly it was to show him the fountain, but they were talking very earnestly in French.

She had wondered then what it could be about.

She knew now that her Stepmother had managed to get the Earl and herself invited to the festivities that were to take place in Sweden on the Prince's birthday.

'She is clever with men,' Lencia thought. 'She twists Papa round her little finger and now she has done the same with the Ambassador. She always gets her own way. It is Alice and myself who are going to suffer.'

They were certainly ignored for the next few days.

The Countess was in a flutter as to what she should wear in Sweden, and which of the magnificent collection of Armeron jewels she should take with her.

She had them all brought up from the safes to her

bedroom and sat trying on the Tiaras one after another.

The diamond set, the emerald set, the sapphire set.

There was also the very pretty turquoise and pearl set which Lencia remembered her Mother wearing and looking like a Fairy Queen.

It was a relief when her Stepmother put it to one side and said:

"I do not like myself in blue."

She did, however, hesitate over the sapphires.

They were an amazing collection which had originally been brought to England from Brazil.

When she put them on, the Countess decided they made her look old.

"*Non, non,*" she said, waving them away. "I want to sparkle, and those purple eyes would haunt me!"

Finally everything was decided.

The Earl was rather surprised at the number of trunks they were taking with them and the vast supply of hat-boxes.

But he agreed with his new wife that they must do England proud.

There were not many English going to Sweden because it was so near the beginning of the London Season.

"That, Dearest, is why they want you," the Countess told the Earl. "And who could represent the Crown and the Union Jack better than someone who is undoubtedly the most handsome man in England today?"

Lencia glanced at her Father to see if this compliment was too creamy for him.

He accepted it with a slight smile, and she told herself her Stepmother was being very clever.

"Now, look after everything while I am gone," the Earl said the night before they left. "And of course keep the horses exercised."

"Of course, Papa," Lencia agreed.

"It will not be the same as having you with us, or going to France with you," Alice said in a dismal little voice.

Her Stepmother was not in the room, but the Earl looked rather nervously towards the door before he said:

"To be honest, my Dearest, I would much rather be going to France. But I could not disappoint your Stepmother, so we all three have to make the best of it."

"Yes, of course," Lencia replied, "and do not worry about us, Papa, we will be all right."

She knew as she spoke that she was speaking for herself, as Alice was looking depressed and dismal.

Then a sudden idea came into her mind.

It was so sensational, she thought she would just laugh it off.

But when she went to bed she was still thinking about it.

"I am crazy! Of course we cannot do such a thing," she told herself.

But the idea did not go away.

She found herself going over it step by step in her mind.

It was just as her Father had taught her to do when they planned something.

The next morning was all excitement and noise.

Her Stepmother, because she was nervous, was speaking sharply to the Servants.

Finally they set off, the Earl and the Countess in one carriage, the Brake coming behind, carrying the mountain of luggage, the French lady's-maid, and the Earl's Valet.

The two girls kissed them goodbye on the steps.

As the carriage went off, they waved.

Their Father was almost leaning out of the window to wave in return.

Then, as the horses disappeared down the drive, Alice turned round and walked through the hall and into the Sitting-Room at the far end of it.

It was where she and Lencia usually sat when they were alone.

"Well, they have gone," she said as her sister came in, "and I hope they enjoy themselves. What are we going to do, I would like to know."

"I can tell you. You and I are going to Chaumont."

Alice stared at her.

"What are you . . . saying?" she asked.

"We are going to Chaumont to see it for ourselves," Lencia repeated. "You know as well as I do that we shall never get there if we wait for Stepmama's approval. So we have just got to be daring and go on our own. And, if you think about it, why not?"

"Why not?" Alice repeated.

There was a lilt in her voice, but she added:

"How can we do it alone?"

"I will tell you exactly," Lencia said again, looking over her shoulder to make sure the door was shut. "We have to be very clever about it, because no-one must know where we are going and we must be back before Papa and Stepmama return from Sweden."

"That gives us ten days," Alice said.

"I know," Lencia replied. "I worked it out last night. Of course we cannot go alone, just two young girls together."

"Then who can we ask to go with us?" Alice enquired.

"You will be accompanied," Lencia said slowly, "by a widowed lady of about twenty-five and her name is Lady Winterton."

Alice stared at her.

"But who . . . ?" Then she gasped, "You cannot mean . . . you?"

"Yes, me," Lencia said. "I have thought it all out. I can wear Mama's clothes because, as you know, we kept them all. They will make me look older, and you will just have to be yourself."

"But surely it is impossible! How can we?" Alice began.

"We have to be brave and we have got to be very careful not to make a mistake," Lencia replied, "but, if I am much older than you and married, I see no reason why I should not take you to France. After all, if things get difficult or we get into trouble, we can always come home."

"I believe you, I believe you!" Alice cried. "Oh, Lencia, you are a genius! I do so want to see Chaumont!"

"I know you do," Lencia said. "I asked myself why Stepmama should spoil everything. She has made Papa happy and that is his business. But we are definitely unhappy and we have every right to fight for ourselves."

"I will fight . . . I am longing to . . . fight," Alice declared.

"Well, we will have to hurry to get everything arranged."

"What have I got to do?" Alice asked.

"Help me choose and pack Mama's clothes, for one thing," Lencia said. "The Housemaids can do yours, but they must not see what I am doing, for otherwise they will talk."

Alice nodded.

"I will not need a lot of clothes, as we will not be staying long," Lencia went on. "But they must make me look older. I shall have to use powder and, of course, a very little rouge, as Mama did when she went to London."

"Mama did not use it in the daytime," Alice remarked.

"No, but Stepmama does," Lencia answered. "She is

'made up to the nines,' but everyone seems to take it as normal. So I imagine that is how all the French women behave."

"Yes, of course they do," Alice said. "I have read about them, and Papa told me once that in Paris the Ladies look like actresses."

"Then that is how I must look as soon as we get away from here," Lencia said. "You must tell the Maids we are going to stay with friends in London, so we will have to get ourselves taken there without anyone from the Stables knowing we are going abroad."

"That is not going to be easy," Alice said.

"I have thought it all out," Lencia said. "We will get our own horses to take us as far as the *Three Kings*."

"Where is that?" Alice asked.

"It is a Posting-Inn where I know Papa changes horses when he is driving to London. If you remember, we changed horses there the last time we went to stay with Uncle Tyson."

"Yes, of course," Alice said, "I remember now."

"I think," Lencia said, "we can cover our tracks better if we drive to London rather than go by train."

Alice said nothing, and Lencia went on:

"It is still early in the morning, so we have all day to make our plans. After spending the night at the *Three Kings*, we will hire a carriage to take us to London. From there we can catch a train to Dover and cross the Channel on the later boat. That will enable us to take the evening Express to Paris."

"How do you know all this?" Alice asked.

"I was working it out for our own trip with Papa before he went to stay in Nice."

She gave a sigh.

"Oh, dear, if only he had not gone! But it seemed

such a good idea at the time for him to get away from everything and cheer himself up."

"I know," Alice said, "but we did not know that would mean Stepmama."

Lencia was about to say something, then thought it was a mistake.

Instead, she said:

"Let us get on with our own plans. We just have to go over them again and again until we are quite certain they are fool-proof. Nothing—I mean nothing—Alice, must go wrong."

chapter two

AFTER luncheon, when they knew the Servants would be busy or resting at the back of the Castle, they went upstairs.

Their Mother's room had been closed ever since she had died.

In fact, the Earl had refused to have anything touched.

When Lencia opened the door, she was immediately vividly aware of her Mother.

There was still the soft fragrance of white violets that she had always used.

It was with difficulty that she did not look towards the bed to see if her Mother was lying back against the pillows, and, at the same time, holding out her arms towards her.

Lencia drew back the curtains, and the sunshine flooded in.

She felt as if at any moment she would hear her Mother

speak to her, and everything would be exactly as it had been a year ago.

When her Mother died, Lencia had asked over and over again in her prayers why it had happened.

"Why did You take her away, God," she pleaded, "when we needed her so desperately?"

She felt now as if in some way she had been cheated out of the most important part of her life.

It was difficult not to hate her Stepmother even more than she did already.

But as she had said to Alice, she knew it was no use fighting against the inevitable.

She had forced herself to remember that nothing would bring her Mother back, and that life had to go on.

No matter how difficult it would be, her Father must not suffer again as he had suffered already.

As it all turned over and over in her mind, it prevented her from crying, though she wanted her Mother so longingly.

Everything in the room told her all too clearly what she had lost.

Then she remembered that the reason she had come here was to help Alice.

It was wrong that Alice should be made so unhappy at not being able to go to France as had been planned.

Ever since her Mother's death, Lencia had been very conscious that Alice had come to her for guidance and help.

Because she was the younger of the two, it was in a way sadder for her to lose her Mother.

Lencia had felt she had to take her Mother's place.

"It will make her happy if we go to France," she told herself, "and whatever Stepmama may do or say, that is where we are going."

Resolutely, but it needed an effort, she opened the wardrobe.

It was filled with her Mother's beautiful day-dresses.

There was another wardrobe in the room next door which contained all the gowns the Countess had worn in the evening.

Alice had not spoken since they had come into the bedroom.

She had just stood looking at the photographs on her Mother's Dressing-Table, at the miniatures which had been painted when they were children, and the large portrait of the Earl.

This hung over the mantelpiece and was her Mother's favourite.

Now, when Alice saw the long row of gowns making a kaleidoscope of colour in the sunshine, she came nearer to her sister.

"Are you really going to wear Mama's gowns?" she asked. "Papa said no-one was to touch them."

"I am going to wear them," Lencia said, "because if I am to chaperon you, I must look old enough to do so."

She spoke fiercely, as if she were fighting someone who was criticising her.

"Now let us choose those which will make me seem a respectable widow who would protect you if you were in any trouble."

"What sort of trouble?" Alice asked interestedly.

"We will find that out soon enough," Lencia said, "but I must be prepared to cope with it. Not as a boring *débutante* but as a Lady getting on in years."

They both laughed.

Lencia lifted down a very pretty gown which was in a deep blue with a little jacket to match it.

"What about this?" she asked.

"It looks rather heavy," Alice replied, "if the weather is going to be hot, as I expect it will be in France."

Lencia thought she had a point there and chose another gown.

It was in a paler blue and the skirt was decorated with frills which were also repeated on the jacket.

"I remember Mama wearing this when she was going to London," she said.

"I think it is very pretty," Alice said. "But you will want more than one."

They went through the wardrobe very carefully.

Finally they chose three very smart dresses which were all suitable, Lencia thought, for an older woman.

They then had to find the hats to go with them.

Fortunately those were also next door in what their Mother had called her "Cupboard Room."

"Now the evening-gowns," Lencia said, "and as we shall be staying in a Hotel, they must not be too grand or too *décolleté*."

They chose two gowns which their Mother had worn when dining at home with the family or with just two or three visitors staying in the House.

Lencia thought she had finished, when Alice said:

"There is a gown in which you would look lovely! You must take it!"

She pointed to one of turquoise-blue chiffons embroidered at the neck and round the edge of the frilly skirt with diamanté.

Lencia remembered how it had glittered when her Mother wore it.

"I should have no use for that," she said. "Remember, we are going to France just as tourists."

"We might be asked to dinner in one of the Castles," Alice said a little wistfully.

"That is very unlikely, as few of them are lived in," Lencia replied.

"Well, bring it just in case," Alice pleaded. "You will look as pretty in it as Mama did, and even if you do not put it on, it will at least have enjoyed the trip abroad, as I shall."

Because it pleased Alice, Lencia put it with her other clothes.

She reckoned that they would stay four or five days.

She therefore added one more simple evening-gown and another day-dress to her collection.

They packed them into a trunk which was fortunately available in the wardrobe room and filled also two hat-boxes.

"We will leave them here until the last moment," Lencia said. "Then we will put them in the corridor outside my room for the footmen to take downstairs. They will not realise they have come from this room and not mine."

Alice agreed that this was sensible.

Lencia had already told her Maid that on this occasion she particularly wished to pack for herself.

She then went to her Mother's Dressing-Table to get what she knew was essential if she was to appear to be at least six or seven years older than she actually was.

She found what she was seeking at the very back of a drawer.

It was a little box that contained a pale but pretty shade of rouge and a salve for the lips.

She remembered her Mother saying that all married women in London used powder and rouge.

"Although I do not need it," she added, "I have no wish to look like a country bumpkin."

"Do you think that will make you look older?" Alice asked.

27

"I hope so," Lencia replied.

She found a box of powder and a powder puff in the same drawer.

There was also a little dark pencil which she thought her Mother must have used on her eyebrows.

She put them into the trunk with her other clothes.

Then she looked round the bedroom to make sure they had left everything as tidy as when they came in.

Alice went out first and ran to her own room to see if the Maid had packed all the gowns she had told her to pack that morning.

Lencia was alone in her Mother's bedroom.

She stood for a moment, looking down at the bed where she had last seen her Mother.

"Perhaps this is wrong, Mama," she whispered, "without telling Papa. But it means so much to Alice to go to France. She has been very brave since you left us, and needs a holiday away from the Castle. So please do not be angry with me."

As she finished speaking, she felt as if her Mother were near her and a hand was touching her forehead.

It was, she told herself, just a fancy, but at the same time it seemed very real and a fear came into her eyes.

"We will not do anything, Mama, of which you would disapprove," she said softly, "but we cannot just sit here feeling miserable because Papa has gone to Sweden and nobody is interested in us."

Again she thought her Mother understood.

Then, because she was afraid of bursting into tears, she went from the room, shutting the door and locking it behind her.

Now everything had been packed.

Even a number of the books that Alice had collected so carefully from the Library had been included in her trunk.

It was then that Lencia remembered that they would need money.

She was so used to travelling with her Father, who saw to everything, including personal tips, that it had not occurred to her until then that she would have to pay all the costs of their journey.

"Money!" she said to her sister. "We have forgotten that!"

"I did think about it," Alice replied, "but I thought you must have lots."

"I have got very little left from my pocket-money," Lencia said, "and I expect you have spent all yours."

"I have about two pounds," Alice answered.

"Well, that certainly will not get us to France," Lencia said, "so we must think quickly."

Then she gave a little cry.

"I know, I know what I must do. But we must be very careful to put it all back before Papa discovers what I have done."

"What are you going to do?" Alice asked.

"Papa has often asked me to open for him the safe in his bedroom where he always keeps his money when he is at home. I think we shall have to raid it."

She gave a little frightened cry.

"Unless he is to find out what we have done," she continued, "which I am sure would make him very angry, we must put back every penny we take."

"I expect we shall be able to do that," Alice said. "After all, we can get some money from Mr. Bentley if we give him a convincing reason for needing it."

Mr. Bentley was the Earl's Secretary, who paid the wages of the Household.

He also provided the girls with any cash they needed to go shopping or to buy presents.

"I can ask him for a little money today," Lencia said reflectively. "He will know we are going away, but he has got to think we are just staying with friends in London, as the other Servants have been told."

"Of course," Alice agreed. "But we will need a great deal more than that, enough for tips for the staff and a present for our imaginary hostess."

They both knew this was true.

There was nothing, in fact, that Lencia could do but rob her Father's safe.

She thought she had been very stupid not to calculate from the very beginning what the whole journey would cost.

But she had never had to trouble her mind about this in the past.

The tickets and everything else had appeared like magic when they reached the Station.

It was therefore not surprising that it had not occurred to her.

The curtains were drawn in her Father's bedroom, and they had to pull them back to see their way to the safe.

Now Lencia definitely felt she was doing something wrong.

But there was nothing else she could do except give up the whole idea of going to France.

She was practical enough to realise that it would be disastrous if they ran out of money and had to apply to the British Embassy for help.

It would be very embarrassing.

What was more, they would have to explain why their passports were in one name and they were travelling under another.

Their Father had got them their own passports when

they had planned to go with him to France.

Before that they had been included on his, but he had said:

"You are both old enough now to have your own passports, and I think you should look after them and be careful not to lose them."

Lencia and Alice had been delighted when they had seen their passports signed by the Secretary of State for Foreign Affairs.

She knelt down by the safe which was let into the wall and hidden by a small oak table in front of it.

The Earl's bedroom was one of the show rooms of the Castle.

The huge red velvet bed had been there for generations.

It was ornamented at the back with the Coat of Arms of the Earls of Armeron in colour.

Much of the furniture had also been there for hundreds of years.

The pictures on the wall were portraits of the Earls of Armeron starting with the first Earl in the armour he had worn when serving with King Richard Coeur-de-Lion.

As she operated the code numbers of the combination lock and opened the safe door, Lencia had the feeling that her ancestors were looking down on her disapprovingly.

She almost felt as if they wanted to prevent her from taking the money she needed so urgently.

To her delight, she found there was more money in the safe than she had expected.

At the last moment she had been afraid that her Father would have taken it all with him to Sweden.

But there was a large number of ten-pound and twenty-pound notes and a considerable pile of gold coins.

31

"I think we should take at least one hundred pounds," Alice said in a whisper.

Lencia thought she was whispering because, like her, she thought, their ancestors were watching.

"Surely we shall want more than that," Lencia replied.

In fact, she had really no idea what everything would cost.

She took two hundred and fifty pounds in notes and about twenty gold sovereigns.

Then she shut the safe.

She put back the table in front of it and left the bedroom as quickly as possible.

She felt, as she walked down the passage, that the Earls in their frames were all shaking their heads at what they considered extremely unladylike behaviour.

"Now, have we forgotten anything else?" she asked Alice as they reached her bedroom.

"I hope not," Alice said. "I would have liked to take more books with me, but there was not enough room."

"You can read them when you come back," Lencia said, "and do not forget we have to pay back every penny we have taken from the safe before Papa opens it."

When she went to bed, Lencia went over everything again in her mind to make quite sure she had forgotten nothing.

In fact, she could not sleep because she was so anxious.

She had made all the arrangements for the following morning.

She had told the Chief Groom he was to drive them to where they were going to stay with friends.

The carriage with her Father's fastest and best horses were waiting for them after an early breakfast at seven-thirty.

She and Alice had pulled the boxes out from her Mother's room the last thing before they went to bed.

No-one asked them where they were going for the simple reason there was no-one of any authority in the Castle.

Alice's governess, who would certainly have been curious, had gone on her holidays.

She would not be returning until just before the Earl and the Countess came back from Sweden.

"We are fortunate to have got away without telling many lies," Lencia said to herself.

But she knew that after the night in the *Three Kings* she would be telling what she would feel was a lie with almost every word she spoke.

At the same time, she was well aware how excited her sister was.

"We are off, we really got off," Alice whispered as they went down the drive.

The way she spoke told Lencia that she had been frightened up to the very last minute that something would stop them.

Instead they were on their way, travelling very fast in the light Chaise their Father had specially built for long journeys.

The London road was a good one.

They reached the *Three Kings* quite easily by tea-time, having stopped for nearly an hour for luncheon.

Lencia had explained to the Chief Groom, who was driving them, that their friends were picking them up there.

If he took the horses back slowly they would not be over-tired.

"Ye leave it to me, M'Lady," the Chief Groom replied. "Oi'll not run them off their feet, ye can be sure o' that."

33

"Of course I can," Lencia said, "and thank you very much for driving us so comfortably."

Alice thanked him also, and they went into the *Three Kings*.

It was a large and impressive Posting-Inn.

The Proprietor remembered Lencia from when she had come with her Father.

"'Tis a privilege an' honour to see Your Ladyship again," he said, bowing. "Will you be staying wi' us or just havin' a break on your journey."

"My sister and I would like to stay the night," Lencia said, "and we would also be grateful if tomorrow you could provide us with a fast carriage to take us into London."

The Proprietor looked slightly surprised, although he did not say anything.

He showed them into what Lencia was aware was one of their best bedrooms.

Her Father had occupied it the last time they had come here.

Because she thought it wise in case anyone who knew them happened to be in the Inn, they had dinner in a private room, although it cost more.

In fact, when Lencia saw what she had to pay for their bedroom and their dinner, she was glad she had taken as much money as she had from the safe.

The carriage which conveyed them to the Station in London was also expensive.

As her Father had always done, she gave the Driver a good tip.

When she came downstairs in the morning, she had hurried through her goodbyes to the Proprietor.

She hoped he would not notice how different she looked from when she had arrived.

However, as he was an elderly man and wore spectacles, she thought he would not notice.

She had put on one of her Mother's gowns and packed the one in which she had arrived.

She put on a hat of her Mother's and felt as if everyone would be staring at her.

She had rather cheated on her face, using only a very little powder and not adding the salve to her lips.

"I will put that on later," she told herself.

Alice, of course, noticed the difference immediately.

"You do look older," she said when they were seated in the Posting-Carriage. "In fact, I would think you were getting on for thirty rather than a girl of not yet twenty."

"I hope everyone thinks the same," Lencia said, "and I must carry myself in a very dignified way. I am just wondering if it would have been wiser if I had said you were my daughter."

Alice laughed.

"I think that would be straining their credulity. To tell the truth, Lencia, you look very, very pretty, just as I remember Mama looked lovely in that hat."

"Well, remember from now on that I am Lady Winterton," Lencia said, "and your name is Austin."

"Alice Austin does not sound too bad," Alice said, "and thank goodness we have not changed our Christian names, otherwise I would never remember."

"It is very important we do not make a mistake," Lencia said.

She repeated this as they finally reached the Station.

Then the luggage was taken from the carriage by a Porter.

As he moved away, after asking what train they were travelling on, Lencia stopped him.

"One moment," she said. "I am afraid I forgot to put the labels on our luggage. Would you be very kind and tie them on for me?"

She handed them to him as she spoke.

On three of them, boldly written in black ink was "Lady Winterton," and on the other two "Miss Alice Austin."

The Porter obligingly tied them on the different trunks and hat-boxes.

There were three of the latter, because Alice had one too.

Lencia tied another onto the basket she carried which contained some food for them to eat on the train.

She thought it would be a mistake to go to the Restaurant Car.

Alice also had a hand-case on which she tied a label.

This she had packed herself.

Lencia knew that it contained a number of books on the Castles of the Loire and especially on Chaumont.

Alice had talked so much about the Castles.

Now that they were actually on their way towards them Lencia was afraid she might be disappointed when they reached Chaumont.

The Porter was impressed by her title and found them a compartment marked "Ladies Only" which was empty.

"Ye be early, M'Lady," he said. "Oi'll try an' get the Guard to lock yer in, in case there be a large crowd at th' last moment."

"That will be very kind," Lencia replied.

She gave him a tip.

As he thanked her profusely, she wondered if it had been too large.

He kept his word, and the Guard came and locked them in.

They were thankful that he had done so, because five minutes later what seemed to be a whole school descended on the platform.

They were a noisy collection of teen-agers.

The people who were with them and the Porters were having difficulty in preventing them from invading every carriage, whether it was 1st, 2nd, or 3rd class.

Finally they were accommodated in 3rd class carriages.

A large number of other passengers got onto the train as well.

"We are lucky to be on our own," Alice said.

"I never expected there would be such a crowd," Lencia replied, "but now we can eat our luncheon in peace as soon as you feel hungry."

She herself was still too agitated and apprehensive to want to eat anything.

However the barley-water they had brought with them seemed delicious, and there was also some fruit.

The train took longer than they had expected to reach Dover.

Every time they stopped, Alice was afraid something had gone wrong and they might not catch the late afternoon boat to Calais.

"I am sure it will wait for the train with all these people on it," Lencia said soothingly.

"It would be no use waiting if the train had broken down, and trains do break down," Alice answered. "I have read about it in the newspapers."

Lencia laughed.

"The newspapers tell you only when things go wrong, never when they go right. I am quite sure, Alice, that as all has gone well so far, we are going to be lucky."

"I do hope so," Alice replied.

They actually reached Dover punctually.

As they went aboard the ship that was waiting for them, Alice was too happy to speak.

It was a warm day with no wind, and the sea looked very calm.

They saw passengers going down in herds below deck, but Lencia decided she would rather sit outside for as long as it was possible.

Alice thought the same.

They found two comfortable chairs from which, as the ship sailed, they could see the White Cliffs of Dover.

"We have done it! We have really done it!" Alice cried. "I thought last night that something was bound to stop us at the last moment."

"Well, your wish has come true," Lencia said, "and we cannot ask for more."

"I am going to ask for a great deal more," Alice declared. "I want to see every Castle in the Loire Valley before I go home."

"That might take you years," Lencia protested, "and think of the commotion if Papa comes home and finds us not there!"

Alice laughed.

"It would serve him right for being so unkind and breaking his word to us."

"Perhaps one day we will tell him how clever we have been in going to France without him," Lencia said. "But just for the moment, let us not count our chickens before they are hatched, and we must make sure we do not make any mistakes."

The ship had been under way for some time when Lencia was aware there was a man looking at her and Alice with curiosity.

He was walking round and round the deck, as a number of other men were doing.

In fact, he passed several times, but each time drew a little nearer to where they were sitting.

Also, she thought, he moved a little more slowly.

He was certainly not English, possibly French.

He was dark, not particularly tall, and seemed, she thought, to be about forty years old.

He was dressed very elegantly with a cape over his shoulders which she knew the smartest men affected when they were travelling.

She was aware of him for some time before Alice said:

"Who is that man who keeps looking at us? Do you think he knows who we are?"

"I hope not," Lencia said. "I am sure I have never seen him before."

"He keeps looking and staring at us," Alice said nervously, "in a funny sort of way."

Lencia thought it was perhaps because they were two women travelling alone.

Then, as the stranger came round for the fourth—or was it the fifth?—time, he stopped.

Lifting his hat, he spoke to Lencia, saying:

"Forgive me for introducing myself, but I am the *Comte* de Pontlevoy and I am sure I have met your husband, Lord Winterton, on several occasions."

Lencia looked up at him, realising she had been right and he was French.

He spoke English very well however, with only a slight accent.

For a moment she could not think what to say, then in a low voice she replied:

"My . . . husband . . . is dead."

"I am very sorry to hear that," the *Comte* replied. "I always found him a charming and very interesting man. I had no idea he was married."

Lencia was wondering frantically how she should reply.

Then she was aware the *Comte* was not looking at her but at Alice.

She was looking very pretty in a green travelling gown which was a perfect frame for her translucent skin.

It also accentuated the colour of her hair, which was dark like her Father's.

There was no doubt that Alice was extremely pretty.

She was only at the moment over-shadowed by Lencia, who with her Mother's beauty left those meeting her for the first time speechless.

Without waiting for an introduction, the *Comte* held out his hand to Alice.

"I am sure you are enjoying the sea voyage," he said. "Is it your first?"

"Yes, it is," Alice replied, "and I am finding it very exciting."

"It is something I always enjoy," the *Comte* replied. "You must tell me what are your first impressions, because that is something one never forgets."

As he spoke he moved from standing in front of Lencia and sat down on a chair beside Alice.

As he did so, he knocked against the bag which she had put at her feet.

Lencia had done the same with hers.

Now she understood, almost as if it had been pointed out to her, how the *Comte* had managed to introduce himself.

She had put at her feet the basket in which she had carried their food.

Its label was hanging from the handle to which it had been tied, and would have been easily readable by those passing by.

The *Comte,* if indeed he was one, had wanted an excuse to speak to them.

She had provided it, very stupidly, she now thought.

"We are on our way to Blois," Alice was saying, "because we are going to Chaumont, which is something I have longed to see for years."

"Then I shall have the pleasure of seeing you there," the *Comte* said, "because I live quite close to Chaumont. In fact, I am returning there now after a visit to friends in England."

"Then you know the Castle well?" Alice enquired. "Is it as beautiful as it sounds?"

"Even more beautiful," the *Comte* replied, "and I hope I shall have the pleasure of showing you round."

There was something in the way he spoke which made Lencia feel uneasy.

He had forced an introduction for himself, she was quite certain of that.

Now he was making arrangements to show Alice round Chaumont.

She wondered quickly what she should do.

Picking up the hamper at her feet, she said:

"I am feeling rather cold, Alice. I think we should go below. It would be a great mistake to catch a chill."

"Yes, of course," Alice replied immediately. "But this gentleman is telling me about Chaumont."

With her head in the air and walking with what she hoped was dignity, Lencia walked away.

There was nothing Alice could do but follow her.

"I will see you again," the *Comte* said as she rose to her feet. "You can be quite certain of that. We will talk about the beauty of Chaumont and, of course—yours."

Alice looked at him wide-eyed.

She was not quite certain that he had said the last words, but if he had, they seemed to her very strange.

"I must go after my sister," she said quickly.

Picking up her bag of books, she hurried after Lencia.

The *Comte* sat, watching her go, a smile on his lips.

Alice caught up with Lencia just as she was going down into the Saloon.

"Why did you go away like that?" she asked. "The *Comte* who spoke to us lives near Chaumont."

"He may do so or he may not," Lencia said. "He picked us up in a blatant way by pretending he knew my husband, who you know as well as I do does not exist."

"There may be a Lord Winterton for all we know," Alice retorted.

"What I do know," Lencia replied, "is that the *Comte* read the name on the label I very stupidly put on this basket, and thought it was a good way to make our acquaintance."

Alice stared at her in astonishment.

"Do you really think that is what he did?"

"I am quite certain of it," Lencia said, "and it would be a great mistake, Darling, for you to know men like that."

Alice said nothing.

She thought as they found a place to sit below that she would much rather have been on deck talking to the *Comte* about Chaumont.

But of course Lencia was right: they must not talk to strange men.

After all, he might be a crook.

She could not, however, help looking for him when they reached Calais.

It was getting dark and the dim lights seemed to make it more difficult to see.

Just as they were getting into the Express train for Paris, Alice heard a voice behind her.

It was the *Comte:*

"Do not forget me, Miss Austin," he said. "We will meet at Chaumont and I will tell you fascinating things about it which other people are unable to do."

"Oh, thank you, thank you," Alice said, "I hope you will not forget."

"You can be quite certain I shall not," the *Comte* replied.

Alice smiled at him.

Then, as she realised that Lencia had gone ahead of her into the train, she hurried up the steps to follow her.

They had a sleeping carriage to themselves and the beds were already made up.

"I have never slept in a train before," Alice said, "it is very exciting."

"What did that man say to you?" Lencia asked in a cold voice.

"He said he would see me in Chaumont and tell me lots of things that other people could not tell me," Alice replied. "That is what I want to hear, Lencia, and it is no good being too disagreeable towards him, or we shall be left just to the guides."

"I do not trust him," Lencia said. "And we have to be very careful whom we talk to on this journey, as we have no man to protect us."

Alice did not answer, thinking her sister was being unnecessarily prudish.

There could not be any harm in speaking to a *Comte*, especially if he was talking about Chaumont.

chapter three

THE train arrived in Paris at seven o'clock the next morning.

A steward had told Lencia that she must be in no hurry to get off at once, as it stayed at the platform for nearly two hours.

But because Lencia had no wish to see the *Comte* again, she insisted that she and Alice leave almost as soon as the train arrived.

She had deliberately not gone at dinner time to the Restaurant Car which was attached to the train.

She knew it would be impossible there to avoid the *Comte*.

She had instead asked a steward to bring some food to their compartment.

They also ate the remainder of the fruit and some home-made cake from her basket.

Alice thought Lencia was being very fussy about the

Comte but decided it wise to say nothing.

They found a Porter to collect their luggage, and a fiacre took them from the *Gare du Nord* to the *Gare Montparnasse*.

Here they were lucky.

Although they were early, a train for Blois was in the Station, and they found themselves a comfortable compartment.

"Now we are on the last lap of our journey," Alice said delightedly.

She opened her bag and took out a book about Chaumont to read extracts from it to her sister.

"Those are all the things I want to see," she said, "and I hope there will be someone to show me the places that are not open to the ordinary members of the public."

Lencia knew that she really meant the *Comte*, but thought it best not to argue about it until the occasion arose.

She was quite certain in her mind that the *Comte* was an undesirable acquaintance.

However, she knew she had no valid reason for saying so.

"I just instinctively feel that he is unpleasant," she told herself.

She remembered how her Mother had always said she had an instinct as to whether a person was nice or nasty.

It was not what they said or did, but what they were.

They seemed to have been waiting for a long time in the *Gare Montparnasse* before finally the train began to move.

They had not been locked in their compartment as they had been in England.

Two other passengers had stepped in at the last moment.

One was an elderly man who shut his eyes and went to sleep.

The other was a woman with a small dog which she held in her lap.

They did not, to Lencia's relief, seem interested in her and Alice.

Very quietly Alice continued to read extracts from her book about Chaumont.

It was not a long journey.

Before they arrived they passed through some very beautiful country and there were some *Châteaux* to be seen in the distance.

Alice got more and more excited.

"Look, Lencia," she kept saying, "there is a *Château* amongst the trees. I wonder if it is in my book, but I am not quite certain where we are."

Her excitement made her look even prettier than usual.

Lencia thought she must be careful and protect her from men like the *Comte*.

It was something she had not anticipated when she planned their journey to France.

She still thought of her sister as being quite young, still in the Schoolroom.

The idea of there being any danger from men had never occurred to her.

Now, for the first time, she thought that perhaps she would have been wiser to wait and hope that their Father would take them when he had time.

But she was sure it would have meant that Alice would have continued to be disappointed.

That did seem unfair, especially when they had spent all last year in heavy gloom, in mourning for their Mother.

Alice had missed her more than anyone else did, except, of course, her Father.

It had not helped when they received no invitations from their friends, who thought they were being tactful.

Lencia was quite sure also that people generally avoided those who were in mourning.

It made them feel depressed too.

Everyone had to die sooner or later, but there was no doubt that the majority looked on death with horror.

It was something that they did not wish to think about until it happened.

When the train came into Blois, Alice was almost jumping for joy.

"We are here! We are here!" she cried. "I was so certain something would prevent us from actually arriving."

"Well, thank goodness, you were wrong," Lencia said. "Now let us get our luggage and try to find somewhere to stay before you rush off to see the Castles."

They got out of the carriage onto the platform.

The Station was not very large, but there was no sign of a Porter.

They walked to the end of the train.

Here they found one old and rather decrepit-looking Porter very slowly pulling luggage out of the van.

Lencia looked at it and saw that it was packed full.

There was not only passengers' luggage but also a number of large wooden crates which looked very heavy.

In her excellent French she said to the Porter:

"We have two trunks in the van. Would you be kind enough to get them out?"

"I've got to move what's in front of 'em first," he answered in a surly voice.

"But that will take ages," Alice protested.

Lencia was also certain that the Porter would not be strong enough to move the crates himself.

There were one or two smaller pieces of luggage at the side of them.

Passengers picked up their own baggage and walked off with it, not waiting for any help from the Porter.

Too late Lencia realised that, since they had arrived at the Station in Paris so early, their luggage had been put into the back of the van.

With only one elderly Porter, it would be impossible to extract it for what might be a long time.

"I do not know what we can do," she said to Alice.

"But we must get our things out, Lencia, we must!" Alice said. "Shall I climb in to see if I can find them at the back?"

"No, of course not," Lencia answered. "Besides, even if you find them, you can hardly lift them out yourself."

"But we must do something," Alice said desperately.

It was then a voice behind them said in English:

"I wonder if I can help you, Ladies?"

Lencia turned round.

Standing just behind them was an extremely handsome gentleman.

In fact, he was so good-looking that she could not help staring at him in astonishment.

Then she realised also that he was smartly dressed and had a noticeable air of authority about him.

"We caught the train early," she said, "and I am afraid our trunks are right at the back of the Guard's van behind those crates. There does not seem anyone capable of collecting them for us."

The man talking to them looked into the van, then turned round.

Behind him Lencia saw there were two Servants wearing very smart uniforms.

He spoke to them, then turned back to Lencia and said in English:

"My Servants will find your luggage if you will be kind enough to tell them what they are to look for."

"Thank you very much," Lencia said.

Speaking in French, she explained there were two trunks and three hat-boxes.

"They are labelled," she added, "Lady Winterton and Miss Alice Austin."

The Servants moved towards the Guard's van, and the Gentleman who had spoken to them said as they went:

"I must apologise for blocking the van with the crates which are being taken to my *Château*."

"They are certainly too heavy," Lencia replied, "for my sister and me to move."

The Gentleman smiled, and Alice said:

"Thank you very, very much for helping us. We might have had to wait here for ages, and I want to hurry up and see the *Châteaux*, which is why we have come here."

The Gentleman smiled again.

"It is for that reason that most people come to Blois, and I hope you enjoy them.

"I am sure we shall," Alice said, "I have read so much about them and they all sound too wonderful to be true."

Then they all three stood watching the Gentleman's Servants as they moved one of the crates out of the van and pushed another to one side to reach the luggage which was at the back.

While they were doing so, passengers kept coming up and taking away their belongings.

It made it easier when Lencia's trunk was found to bring it out onto the platform.

Alice's came next, and then the three hat-boxes.

Lencia gave a sigh of relief.

"Thank you, thank you very much," she said, "you have been very kind and we are most grateful."

One of the servants had produced a trolley and lifted the luggage onto it.

"I presume," the Gentleman said, "you want a carriage. Where are you staying?"

Lencia hesitated.

Then, because he had been so kind, she said:

"I wonder if you could give me the name of a quiet and respectable Hotel. As you have heard from my sister, we are here to see the *Châteaux*."

"I am afraid a great number of people come for the same reason," the Gentleman replied. "So the few Hotels there are in this area are usually overbooked."

Lencia drew in her breath.

She had not thought, which was perhaps very foolish of her, that they should book their accommodation before they arrived.

Alice gave a little cry.

"But we must be near Chaumont," she said. "I want to spend lots and lots of time there, and it may be difficult if we have to stay far away from it."

She looked up pleadingly at the Gentleman.

"Please think of a Hotel which is near to Chaumont."

The Gentleman hesitated, and then he said:

"Perhaps I should introduce myself. I am the *Duc* de Montrichard and, as it happens, the Guardian of Chaumont."

Alice gave a little gasp of excitement and stared at him wide-eyed.

"I am afraid," he said, "you are going to find it extremely difficult to find accommodation in any hotel. May I therefore invite you as my guests to my own *Château*, which is not far away."

Alice gave a cry of excitement.

But Lencia quickly said:

"We could not accept, *Monsieur*, to be an encumbrance on you, although it is extremely kind of you to suggest it."

"You would not be an encumbrance," the *Duc* replied. "As I have only just returned from spending some time in Paris, there is, I assure you, plenty of room in my *Château* to accommodate you and your sister."

"Oh, thank you, thank you," Alice said before Lencia could speak. "It would break my heart if I could not see Chaumont after coming all this way."

"Then that is something we must prevent at all costs," the *Duc* said with a smile. "So let us get into my carriage, which is waiting outside, and my Servants will follow with your luggage."

Without waiting for Lencia to speak, he gave instructions for the Servants to bring the luggage.

The crates were to be fetched later.

Then he walked down the platform with Lencia on one side of him and Alice on the other.

"I feel very embarrassed," Lencia said, "thrusting ourselves upon you like this."

"You are doing nothing of the sort," he said. "As I have told you, I am not having a house-party at the moment, and you will find only my nephew, the *Vicomte* Béthune, waiting for us at Richard."

"It has been a dream of my sister's for years to see the Castles on the Loire," Lencia said. "We have come very unexpectedly and in a hurry, which is my only excuse for not being sensible enough to book our Hotel accommodation before we left."

"Well, I promise you that your sister shall see all the secret parts of Chaumont which are not open to the public," the *Duc* said, "and she could not do that without my authority."

"That is what the *Comte* de Pontlevoy promised," Alice said impulsively. "But Lencia did not believe he was telling the truth."

"Pontlevoy!" the *Duc* exclaimed. "How do you know that man?"

"We do not know him," Lencia said quickly. "He quite blatantly picked us up on the boat because he saw our names on the labels of our hand-luggage."

"That is the sort of thing he would do," the *Duc* answered. "I advise you, Madame, to have nothing to do with him."

"You are telling me exactly what I thought instinctively," Lencia said, "but my sister in her innocence said she was very interested in Chaumont, and he promised to show her all the things that the ordinary visitor does not see."

"Which is not in his power to do," the *Duc* said loftily. "Unfortunately, he lives in this neighbourhood, but he is a man I should not recommend as a suitable companion for a—young girl."

He glanced at Alice as he spoke.

Lencia thought she understood exactly what he was implying.

"Then I am very grateful, *Monsieur*," she said, "that you have warned us against him, for I am quite certain he intends to be a nuisance where my sister is concerned."

"He is notorious for that," the *Duc* said in a low voice.

Lencia drew in her breath.

She knew now that they had had a very narrow escape.

It had been very silly of her not to realise that there were unpleasant men who were attracted by young girls.

No-one could look prettier than Alice looked at the moment.

Outside the Station there was an open carriage drawn by two extremely fine horses.

The *Duc* helped them into it and there was room for all three of them on the back seat.

He sat between them, saying that he would explain to Alice the *Châteaux* they passed on the way to his own.

"It is very, very exciting for me," Alice said, "and please will you make it possible for me to see as many *Châteaux* as we can before we have to go home. But of course the most important and the most exciting and the one I have dreamed about is Chaumont."

She spoke so eagerly and so excitedly that Lencia thought the *Duc* must be impressed by her sincerity.

"My sister," she said, "has read every book in our Library about Chaumont."

"Where do you live?" the *Duc* asked.

His quite natural question took Lencia by surprise.

She had not thought that she would have to explain to anyone where she lived.

She certainly could not say Armeron Castle, which she was sure would be known even in France.

Thinking quickly, she replied:

"I have a house in London, and also one in Kent."

"And your husband is not with you," the *Duc* said.

"I am a widow," Lencia replied.

"Forgive me," he said, "but you seem too young to be bereaved."

Lencia thought it was best not to reply to this.

She merely looked ahead and then as they crossed a bridge she asked:

"Is this really the River Loire we have just crossed?"

"It is indeed," the *Duc* answered.

"It looks very lovely," Lencia said, "in the sunshine."

"So will Chaumont, which you will see in a moment," the *Duc* replied.

They drove on, and a few minutes later they came in sight of Chaumont.

It was lying a little below them, and at the sight of it Alice gave a cry of sheer delight.

"It is just as beautiful as I expected it to be," she said.

The *Duc* ordered the carriage to come to a standstill.

As Alice stared at Chaumont with its four towers, the *Duc* said with a smile:

"It has four hundred rooms, fourteen great staircases, seven minor ones, and three hundred and sixty-five fire-places."

Lencia laughed, but Alice said:

"I want to see them all, every one of them."

"I am afraid that would take a very long time," the *Duc* said. "But I promise that you will see not only the best of Chaumont, but parts that are not open to the public and for which only I have the key."

"Oh, thank you . . . thank you!" Alice cried. "Can we start now?"

Lencia spoke before the *Duc* could answer.

"No, of course not! *Monsieur le Duc* wishes to return to his own *Château*."

Alice knew it was a rebuke.

"I am very sorry," she said. "It is all so exciting, and even more exciting now that we have met you."

"That is the sort of compliment that I like," the *Duc* replied with a twinkle in his eyes.

"But I do mean it," Alice said, "because now we shall

not have to trail around with a group of sightseers, and you promised I shall see the secret places where no-one else is allowed! Oh! I am so glad we came!"

"So am I," the *Duc* said.

He was answering Alice, but he was looking at Lencia.

As she met his eyes, she suddenly felt shy.

She had the feeling that he was looking at her not exactly with admiration, but in a way which seemed somehow more intimate.

Then she told herself she was a widow woman of a certain age.

Therefore a man like the *Duc* would feel more at home with her than he would with a young girl or a *débutante*.

She remembered her Father saying once that when he was a young man he avoided *débutantes*.

Like all his contemporaries, he was afraid he would be married off to one of them by some ambitious Mama.

"I therefore," he had said, "spent my time with married women who were very beautiful and very amusing but who could not tie me to them with a wedding-ring."

"But you married Mama," Lencia said.

"I fell in love with your Mother the moment I saw her," the Earl replied. "She was the most beautiful person I had ever seen in my whole life. I was determined to get to know her, and as soon as we were introduced, I knew I was really in love."

His voice had deepened as he went on.

"And she miraculously fell in love with me. It was the great romance of the season and, as you know, we lived happily ever after."

Lencia thought now that the *Duc* if he was unmarried, would, like her Father, be avoiding *débutantes*.

'In which case,' she thought, 'as he supposes I am so

much older, we should be able to talk to each other without any difficulty.'

She knew now why she had been aware, before he told her who he was, that there was an aura of importance about him.

Then, when she saw his *Château*, she could understand it even more clearly.

Richard was magnificent.

Even Alice, who was bemused by Chaumont, could not help thinking it was overwhelming.

They turned up a long drive, rising all the time, higher and higher.

They were to learn later that Richard had been built on the site of a former feudal Castle.

It had ruled and protected the countryside which lay beneath it.

Richard had a central pavilion in the Renaissance style and a huge tower with a dome.

The exterior was very impressive.

But Lencia knew the moment she stepped inside that the *Duc* lived in great luxury and his Castle was also a Palace.

They entered a great hall in which there were on duty a number of Servants in the *Duc*'s livery.

A young man came running down the stairs.

"You are back, Uncle Valaire!" he exclaimed. "Did the crates arrive safely?"

"Quite safely, Pierre," the *Duc* replied. "They are on their way here, and I have brought two guests who want our help in seeing all the *Châteaux*."

Pierre was, Lencia thought, a very good-looking young man of about twenty-one or twenty-two.

Then he was bowing respectfully in front of her.

"This is my nephew, the *Vicomte* Béthune," the *Duc*

was saying. "Pierre, this is Lady Winterton and her sister, Miss Alice Austin."

Pierre kissed Lencia's hand, as was correct, and shook hands with Alice.

"It was clever of my Uncle to find you," he said, "as well as the crates which have arrived from Paris after some delay."

"I do hope we are the more important," Alice said. "But we are very grateful to the crates because it was really they who introduced us to your Uncle."

"That is true," the *Duc* said, "and now that we have visitors, I am sure they are as hungry as I am for luncheon."

"You are so late," Pierre replied, "that I very nearly ate it all, but it is in fact waiting for you in the Dining-Room."

The Dining-Room was as magnificent as the rest of the *Château*.

As they ate, the *Duc* told them a little about important visitors who had in the past stayed in Richard, also the names of those great men who had contributed to the treasures in it.

It was only a light meal.

When they had finished, Alice looked at the *Duc* beseechingly, and it was impossible for him not to understand.

"I know what you are asking," he said. "You want to go to Chaumont."

"Oh, please, please, if I can go just for a few minutes," Alice begged. "Having waited so long, I feel I cannot wait until tomorrow."

"Really," Lencia admonished. "I think you are asking too much of *Monsieur le Duc* after he has been so kind to us."

"Chaumont is fortunately only a few minutes drive away," the *Duc* said, "and we will go there at once so that Alice can sleep peacefully tonight. Otherwise I am sure she will stay awake, fearing that it will vanish before the morning."

"That is exactly why I want to go there now," Alice said.

The *Duc* looked at Lencia.

"Will you come too?" he asked. "Or are you too tired?"

"Of course I am not too tired," Lencia laughed.

Then she remembered she was supposed to be older and said in explanation:

"I live mostly in the Country, and I assure you we are far more energetic there than those who live in London."

"I am quite prepared to believe you," the *Duc* said, "so we will all go to Chaumont, and if our legs ache after climbing all those staircases, we can blame your sister."

Alice laughed and Pierre said:

"I will race you up them and I am quite certain I shall win."

"And I shall make sure you do not," Alice retorted. "Like all men, you think women are weak little things who faint at the idea of having to climb a staircase. At this moment I am quite ready to climb to the top of the tower and dance on top of it."

They laughed at this.

But Lencia knew that it was worth all the difficulties they had been through to see her sister so happy.

It was, as the *Duc* had said, only a short drive from his *Château* to Chaumont.

When they arrived there, he took them in through a door to which he alone had the key.

They were in a part of the Castle where visitors were not admitted.

"I am going to show you only a few of the most important things today," he said. "Tomorrow we will take very much longer, that is, if you are still interested."

He was teasing Alice, but she said:

"Of course I will be interested. I cannot tell you how excited I am at being here and seeing this wonderful Castle."

She put out her arms as she spoke almost as if to embrace Chaumont itself.

Alice had told the *Duc* what she most wanted to see, so he took them first to the bedrooms of the two rival owners of Chaumont, Diane de Poitiers and Catherine de Medici.

He also showed them the bedroom of the Astrologer Ruggieri, an inveterate plotter and the Queen's evil adviser.

There were some beautiful pieces of furniture and tapestries dating from the Renaissance period.

Alice also saw the letter "D" which Diane de Poitiers had ordered to be carved on the parapet.

She put out her hand and touched it very gently.

They all knew how much it meant to her.

Then they went to the Royal apartments of King François I.

There was a great deal to admire there.

While Alice and Pierre were looking at something else, the *Duc* showed Lencia the famous lines the King was supposed to have had engraved on a window in his Study.

"Woman is fickle/Mad is he who relies on her."

Lencia read it, and then she said:

"Is that what you believe?"

"It is what I have found in one way or another," the *Duc* replied.

"Then you must have been looking in the wrong place," Lencia said. "Not all women are fickle, and, although there are some on whom no sensible man should rely, they are, I would like to believe, the exception."

She was thinking of her Stepmother as she spoke.

Then she was aware the *Duc* was watching her.

"So you have found women you do not trust," he said. "Was your husband unfaithful to you?"

Because she had forgotten that she was supposed to have had a husband, Lencia looked at him in surprise.

Then she looked away.

"That is not the sort of question," she said, "that you should ask me."

"Why not?" the *Duc* enquired.

As she did not answer, he said after a moment:

"You are very beautiful, Lady Winterton, and I cannot believe any man would be so foolish as to leave you for another woman, even if she were as lovely as Aphrodite herself."

Because she was not used to compliments, Lencia felt herself blush.

She had been very careful when they washed before luncheon to powder her face.

She also applied a little of the rouge on her cheeks.

She had made herself up very carefully before they left the train, in case they encountered the *Comte*.

She felt that if she looked older, she could make it clear to him he was to leave Alice alone.

Now, as she felt her cheeks burn, she turned her head away, and the *Duc* said:

"Many times I have been in England and I have never, and this is the truth, seen anyone as beautiful as you.

Where have you been hiding yourself? When your husband was alive, did he keep you locked up like an Eastern woman so that no other man could ever see you?"

"I have always lived mostly in the Country," Lencia said. "Therefore, the things you are trying to talk about have not come into my life."

"Then you have been very fortunate," the *Duc* said. "The people who have suffered have been those who have been unable to see you, until, of course, now."

There was a note in his voice which told her that he was flirting with her.

Lencia thought she must be careful not to take it seriously.

She had always been told that Frenchmen flirted with every woman they met.

She told herself she would be very stupid if she listened to what the *Duc* said or thought he was at all serious.

'It is the way he would talk to any woman he is with,' she thought. 'It is only because I am English that I find it embarrassing.'

She remembered her Father saying once when he was talking to her Mother about someone they knew:

"Hardly any English woman knows how to accept a compliment."

"Does that refer to me?" the Countess had asked.

"Never, my Precious," the Earl had answered. "You know as well as I do that every man you meet pays you compliments and you receive them modestly, sweetly, and with an irresistible sense of humour. It tells them infuriatingly that you do not believe they are serious."

"I believe your compliments," the Countess said.

"Of course you do," the Earl answered, "because you know they come from my heart. I can only go on saying a thousand times there is no-one in the world as beautiful as you."

They looked at each other lovingly and forgot that Lencia was listening to them.

She had been about twelve at the time, and it was a conversation she had never forgotten.

She thought now that she must behave the same way as her Mother had, enjoying any compliments she was paid, but at the same time, unless they came from someone she loved, not taking them at all seriously.

She looked at the *Duc*.

She was aware that he was watching her with an expression in his eyes that made her feel shy.

"How is it possible you can be so beautiful?" he asked. "I thought as you stood there you might have been Diane de Poitiers herself. You will remember she was the most beautiful woman in France."

"I am delighted that you think so," Lencia managed to say, "at the same time, I must not allow my head to be turned by compliments from a Frenchman who I am sure is a past-master at paying them."

The *Duc* threw back his head and laughed.

"A perfect answer and a very clever one," he said. "I can assure you, Lady Winterton, that it is quite unnecessary for you to be clever as well as beautiful."

They looked at a few more exciting things in Chaumont.

Then the *Duc* insisted on taking them home.

"I am not going to allow my guests to be so tired," he said, "that they will refuse to entertain at dinner-time two men who will be waiting for them eagerly to come downstairs."

"I am not the least tired," Alice said firmly. "And I shall be getting up very early tomorrow morning so that I can go again to Chaumont."

"I am afraid you will have to wait for us," the *Duc* said, "because Pierre and I want to ride before breakfast. So that meal is postponed until nine-thirty."

"I suppose you have some very fine horses," Alice exclaimed.

"I hope that is what they are," the *Duc* answered.

"Can I see them?" Lencia asked. "I have always heard that French horses are outstanding, and now that you have been competing in some of our races, you have been very successful."

The *Duc* put his hand up to his forehead.

"How could I have been so stupid," he asked, "knowing that you were English, not to take you to the Stables first before we went to Chaumont?"

He was joking, but Alice said:

"Chaumont was more important because we are in France. If we had been in England, it would have been the Stables first."

The *Duc* laughed.

"Now it has to be the Stables second, and I hope that you will both ride with me tomorrow morning."

Alice looked at Lencia and said:

"Oh, Lencia, why did you not think of it? How could you have been so stupid?"

"What has she done wrong?" the *Duc* enquired.

"We did not bring our riding-clothes," Alice said.

"How could we have possibly known," Lencia asked, "that there were horses and a *Duc* waiting for us at Chaumont?"

She spoke in such a despairing tone that the men both laughed.

Then the *Duc* said:

"I am sure my Housekeeper can find something you can wear. I have sisters and nieces who stay here habitually, and I am quite certain they leave behind everything that can possibly be wanted. At seven-thirty in the morning you will be seen only by the horses themselves."

Alice gave a little cry.

"You are wonderful!" she said. "I know you must have stepped straight out of a Fairy Story to help us, because you cannot possibly be real."

"Now at last I have found someone who appreciates me," the *Duc* said, "but I have a feeling it is only cupboard-love."

Alice laughed, and then she said:

"I can only say that we are very, very grateful, and everything is far more exciting than I ever expected."

"Let us hope that continues," the *Duc* said.

When they got back to the Castle they went up to their bedrooms, and Alice said:

"This is so wonderful, Lencia. Are you not glad that we came?"

"I am very glad," Lencia answered. "But we must be careful."

"Why?" Alice enquired.

Lencia glanced to make sure that the door was shut, and then she said:

"We are staying here without a chaperon, which would be very shocking if anyone knew that I was not who I am pretending to be—a widowed lady."

"I never thought of that," Alice remarked. "We will be careful."

"I told the *Duc* just vaguely that I had a house in Kent, where I live."

Alice was still for a moment, and then she said:

"I have a dreadful feeling that when Pierre asked me, I said that it was in Hampshire."

Lencia made a gesture with her hands.

"We can only hope that being French, they will not be particularly interested in the Counties of England. But try not to answer any questions directly."

"They are so nice," Alice said, "and I like Pierre very much. I am sure neither he nor the *Duc* would do anything to hurt us."

"I think that too," Lencia said. "At the same time, the *Duc* is often in England and he may even have met Papa."

"We will be very careful until we leave," Alice promised. "And after that it will not matter."

Lencia did not reply.

She was thinking how terribly shocked her Father and Mother's friends would be if they knew they were staying with the *Duc* de Montrichard unchaperoned.

She did not know anything about him.

She had the feeling he was a very dashing figure who would of course know everyone in the Social World.

"We must be very careful," she said to herself.

At the same time, she was frightened.

chapter four

THE *Duc* was right: his Housekeeper produced riding-clothes both for Lencia and Alice.

They dressed themselves quickly at seven o'clock.

The Housekeeper had even been clever enough to provide boots which fitted them.

As the clothes were very French, Lencia had the happy feeling that they were both looking their best.

She was just leaving her bedroom when she remembered she had not made-up her face and hurried back to do so.

"You look very pretty when your face is painted," Alice said, "and it certainly does make you look older."

"I hope so," Lencia said, "and do not forget I am many years older than you."

Alice laughed.

"I will not forget, and if they ask me, I will say that you are like a very strict Governess."

"We had better hurry," Lencia said, "or we shall be late."

They ran downstairs and found the *Duc* and Pierre in the hall.

"A miracle," the *Duc* said, "two women who are actually on time!"

"If you are surprised, you must be thinking of French women," Lencia replied. "The English are always very punctual where horses are concerned."

"Well, do not let us keep ours waiting," the *Duc* said, and moved towards the door.

The Grooms were holding four horses outside.

Lencia was shown the very well-bred horse she was to ride.

She was certain the *Duc* had chosen it because it was well-trained and she would have no difficulty in riding it.

She did not say anything.

When they reached some flat land after riding through the Park, she urged her horse on.

It was an effort to beat the others, who were all galloping.

She was aware as she did so that the *Duc* was watching her.

When finally they pulled their horses to a standstill, he said:

"I was quite right, I knew, because you are English, you would ride well and also look even more like Diane de Poitiers than when you are on foot."

"You must talk to my sister about Diane," Lencia said. "She is her favourite heroine."

"I am surprised you allow that," the *Duc* replied, "considering she was a Mistress of Henry II."

Lencia smiled.

"One is always allowed a little licence when it comes to history. The Mistresses of Kings somehow have an aura about them which does not exist in real life."

The *Duc* looked at her in surprise, and then he said:

"What about your Prince of Wales?"

For a moment Lencia was nonplussed.

She had forgotten that the Prince of Wales had caused so much gossip and talk, first with his friendship with Lily Langtry, then following several other great beauties his adoration for the Countess of Warwick.

She knew, although she said nothing, that the *Duc* was aware what she was thinking.

After a moment he said:

"Exactly, and hardly a good example to innocent young girls like your sister."

Lencia had a feeling it was a question of "the pot calling the kettle black."

However, she thought to say so would seem too familiar, and she therefore replied:

"You must not believe all you hear about our Royal Family. Any more than we believe all we hear about the gaieties of Paris and the fortunes that are spent on some of your beautiful women."

"*Touché*," the *Duc* said. "I see, Lady Winterton, that you have an answer to everything."

"I am afraid that is not true," Lencia replied, "but you have an answer to everything."

"Perhaps I wanted to see your re-action to the delightful story of Diane and Henry II," the *Duc* said. "She was very feminine and she loved her Protector. With her guidance, France became more prosperous than it had ever been before."

"You must tell all this to Alice," Lencia said.

"I prefer to talk to you," the *Duc* replied. "I think, Lady

Winterton, we will find we have a great many things in common and a great many subjects to discuss."

"At the moment I just want to tell you," Lencia said, "how much I am enjoying this ride. But I am well aware, *Monsieur*, that you chose me a very quiet and docile horse. Tomorrow, if I am going to ride with you again, I would like one with more spirit and more difficult to control."

"Now you are speaking in the way I expected," the *Duc* said. "I did not believe that under that quiet and dignified manner, which, of course, is very impressive, there was not an adventurous little goddess wanting to express herself far more vividly."

Lencia thought he was being uncomfortably perceptive, and that could lead to trouble.

She said a little coldly:

"I try to be just myself and not to pretend to be anything else."

"And yourself is the you I want to meet," the *Duc* said, "because she intrigues me. Yet I feel there are barriers that I somehow have to sweep away or surmount."

Lencia was aware that he was far more astute than she had expected.

She moved her horse forward and started off in a gallop.

She knew it prevented the *Duc* from saying any more.

She had the feeling that while he was flirting with her, he was doing it in rather an unusual way.

He was, in fact, probing to find out more about her.

They rode for an hour through the most beautiful country.

The *Duc* explained that it still harboured a large number of wild animals as it had in the days of François I.

"Stags, wild boar, and deer," he said.

Alice listened when he talked about the game and the hunting.

Yet whenever she could, she looked to see Chaumont in the distance.

It was impossible for the *Duc* and Pierre not to realise that she was counting the hours until she could go back there.

When they arrived back at the Castle, there was a large breakfast waiting for them in the Dining-Room.

They went straight in without changing.

Then, as Alice finished her breakfast first, she said enquiringly:

"What time will we be leaving?"

"I suppose," the *Duc* said, "you are bullying me into taking you to Chaumont again. Very well, go and change and I will get all my keys and bring them with me."

Alice gave him a ravishing smile.

"I knew you would understand," she said. "I cannot waste time on other things."

"No, of course not," the *Duc* agreed, "and Pierre and I will make certain that at the end of the day you are so tired that we can all have a rest tomorrow."

"Now you are being unkind to me," Alice protested.

She ran from the Dining-Room and up the stairs.

Lencia left more slowly, feeling she must behave as an older woman should.

The *Duc* walked with her into the hall.

"Now go and make yourself look even lovelier than you do at the moment," he said. "I want Chaumont to see you."

Lencia laughed.

"I thought it was we who are going to see Chaumont."

"The Castle has seen many Beauties," the *Duc* said, "but I am prepared to wager a large sum of money that the Beauty I will produce today will eclipse them all."

"Be careful, you might lose," Lencia said.

"If you challenge me, I shall double my bet," the *Duc* replied.

Lencia laughed and went upstairs.

As she did so, she thought how enjoyable it was to duel with words as she did with the *Duc*.

It was something she had never been able to do before, except in her imagination.

Her Father, while she adored being with him, did not really like discussing a subject.

He was inclined to turn it into a lecture.

She had a feeling that the *Duc* enjoyed being provocative just to see the re-action of the person to whom he was speaking.

"I will certainly give him a run for his money," she told herself.

The Maid was waiting to help her into one of her Mother's pretty gowns.

As this particular one was in a pale blue, she felt it did not make her look as old as she should appear.

She therefore lifted her hair a little higher and put two small pearl ear-rings into her ears.

They had been left to her by her Grandmother in her Will.

Her Mother had, however, never allowed her to wear them.

"Ear-rings are not right for young girls," she had said.

Lencia had found them when she was packing.

It was actually the ear-rings that made her remember she must have a wedding-ring.

This had meant that once again she had had to go to her Mother's room.

She looked in her Dressing-Table for her jewel-box.

The most important jewels were, of course, kept with the family heirlooms in the safe.

This was guarded at night by one of the footmen who slept in the same room.

Their Mother had kept a number of small jewels which she wore regularly in her Dressing-Table.

It was too much trouble to keep taking them out of the safe.

Lencia found her Mother's wedding-ring.

Fortunately it fitted on to the finger of her left hand almost as if it had been made for her.

There was also a pearl ring, which she thought she would wear in the evening, and a necklace which matched it.

She hesitated about a small but very pretty diamond necklace, thinking as she and Alice were going to a Hotel, she would not need jewels.

Then, just in case it was necessary, she slipped it into her jewel-case.

Now she thought if she wore ear-rings she would look more like the widowed woman she was supposed to be.

They looked impressive under the hat she was wearing, which was trimmed with velvet flowers and two feathers.

When Alice came in to see if she was ready, she exclaimed:

"Oh, you do look lovely! I am sure that the *Duc* will think so."

"He says very flattering things," Lencia said, "and I do not believe any of them. If Pierre flatters you, you must remember that for a Frenchman that is the polite way to behave, and they forget what they have said the moment they have said it."

"I like having compliments," Alice said, "and it is certainly a change from Englishmen, who talk enthusiastically only about fishing and shooting."

Lencia laughed.

"Well, make the best of it while you can," she said, "because we shall soon be back home listening to what a success Stepmama has been in Sweden."

Alice made a face.

"We are sure to have to listen to that, and if anyone exciting comes to the house, we shall doubtless be sent to the Schoolroom and told to stay there."

Lencia thought this was very likely.

She felt it justified her in having brought Alice to France without permission.

"Oh, do come on," Alice was saying. "We are wasting time talking about what we are going to do at home, when we are here in France and the doors of Chaumont are going to open for us."

She went out of the room as she spoke.

Lencia took one last look at herself in the mirror and followed her.

The carriage was waiting for them.

Now the *Duc* and Lencia sat on the back seat while Alice and Pierre sat opposite with their backs to the horses.

They were talking nineteen to the dozen.

Lencia knew all that mattered to Alice was that she was on her way to Chaumont.

When they reached it, the *Duc* took them into it by a different door from the one he had used the previous day.

It was the main section of the Castle and had four great guard rooms laid out in the shape of a Greek Cross.

From there he took them up a staircase with windows which led to a terrace.

From there they were able to see tangled chimneys, dormer windows, newel staircases, steeples, and pepper-pot roofs.

He explained to them that this was once a fantastic vantage point.

From it the Ladies of the Court could watch entertainments like hunts, tournaments, or parades.

"It was used occasionally for Balls," Pierre added.

Alice gave a little cry.

"Oh, do give a Ball!" she said to the *Duc.* "Think how exciting it would be for everyone, and you could watch your guests from here and feel that you were King François bringing the Castle to life."

"I think I would rather give a Ball in my own house," the *Duc* answered. "It is something, Pierre, you and I might consider for later on in the summer."

"I have never been to a Ball," Alice said. "Perhaps if I am still not old enough to come to yours, I can watch it from a place like this."

"If I give a Ball, and you are in France," the *Duc* said, "then you shall be one of my most honoured guests."

Alice jumped for joy.

Then, as she caught Lencia's eyes, she remembered that even if she was invited to the Ball she would not be able to go.

They would never be able to explain to their Father how they were friends of the *Duc's.*

For a moment the excitement went out of her eyes.

She turned without speaking and began to descend from the terrace.

The others followed, and Lencia said nothing.

She was, however, quite certain the *Duc* was aware

that he had somehow trodden on unsafe ground.

It was something he would not forget.

They reached the ground floor.

When they opened the locked door and stepped through it, they found themselves in a part of the Castle that was open to the public.

A number of people were being taken round by a guide.

Behind them and obviously not one of the group was, to Lencia's consternation, the *Comte*.

He saw Alice, who was still a little ahead and walked swiftly towards her.

"Where have you been?" he asked. "I looked for you yesterday and I felt sure I should find you here."

Before Alice could reply, the *Duc*, who had come through the door last, said in a lofty tone:

"Miss Austin was with me, Pontlevoy, and I am showing her the Castle."

The *Comte* started and looked at the *Duc* in a hostile fashion.

"I had promised to show Miss Austin the Castle," he said angrily.

"Which of course you are unable to do," the *Duc* said. "She is seeing with me the locked rooms and parts of the Castle which are not open to the public."

He made the last words sound like a deliberate insult.

The *Comte* said:

"I might have guessed that you would somehow interfere."

"It is not a question of interference," the *Duc* said. "Lady Winterton and her sister are my guests, and I can assure you that they will be well looked after and will need no assistance from anyone else."

"That," the *Comte* said, "is exactly the sort of remark I should expect from *Monsieur Mille-Feuilles*."

It was obvious he had lost his temper and was being offensively rude.

"Then you have not been disappointed," the *Duc* said coldly.

As he spoke, he took Lencia by the arm and moved towards another door to which he had the key.

He unlocked it.

Alice and Pierre followed him and Lencia through it.

The *Duc* then slammed the door intentionally and locked it on the inside.

"I am glad you have got rid of him," Lencia said.

"Perhaps he intends only to be kind," Alice objected, "and he did talk about Chaumont as if he was fond of it."

"I doubt if he would have been so attentive," the *Duc* said, "if you had not been a very pretty young girl. So forget the *Comte*, and I assure you you will never meet him in my house."

Alice did not reply.

A few moments later, when she was racing Pierre up the stairs, Lencia, who was going more slowly, said to the *Duc:*

"Thank you for getting rid of that man. I knew he was horrible as soon as he spoke to us on the boat."

"Forget him," the *Duc* answered. "He dislikes me because I refuse to know him even though he lives in the neighbourhood, and he spreads very unpleasant stories about me which I am glad to say few people believe."

"He called you *Monsieur Mille-Feuilles*," Lencia said. "Why did he do that?"

The *Duc* smiled a little cynically.

"I would have thought that was obvious."

"A thousand leaves," she translated.

"Perhaps he should have said '*Mille-Fleurs*.'"

Lencia thought for a moment, and then she said:

"You mean a thousand women. Is that how they describe you?"

The *Duc* made a gesture with his hands.

"Shall we say there is some slight exaggeration."

There was a silence, and then Lencia said:

"And that makes you happy?"

"I find women very attractive especially if they are beautiful," the *Duc* said. "Can you blame a man for refusing what the Gods offer him?"

"Yet you said," Lencia rejoined, "like King François that 'a woman is fickle.' "

"I think in their way they are as fickle as men," the *Duc* said. "But it is not so easy for them to move from flower to flower as it is for a man."

They had reached a room in which there was some very attractive furniture.

Then almost without thinking what she was doing, Lencia sat down on the sofa.

"Why have you never married?" she asked.

"But I have," the *Duc* replied.

Lencia was surprised, but she did not quite know why.

He had never seemed to her to be like a married man.

"I was married, and of course it was an arranged marriage," the *Duc* said. "As you know, in France it is usual between great families. I was just twenty-one, and was told she was beautiful. When I saw her I admitted she was certainly pretty, but there was something strange about her which I did not quite understand."

Lencia was listening.

She knew by the tone of his voice that it hurt him to speak of what had happened.

"As I said," he went on, "my Father and her Father arranged the marriage. I saw very little of my future bride, and of course never alone until after the wedding."

"Then what happened?" Lencia asked.

"When I was on my honeymoon," the *Duc* said, "my wife, who had been so carefully chosen for me, did not behave normally. She was given to strange fits of screaming which usually ended in her becoming unconscious."

Lencia made a little exclamation of horror, but she did not speak, and the *Duc* continued:

"At first they occurred no more than once a month, then became more frequent. I sent for the Doctors, who informed me that my wife was in fact mentally deranged. I also learned that her parents had known about it before they arranged the marriage."

Lencia gave a cry.

"But how terrible! How could they do such a thing?"

"They wanted her to become the Duchess of Montrichard, and nothing else was of any importance."

"It was ghastly for you," Lencia said. "What did you do about it?"

"Because I was ashamed of being duped, I tried to keep it a secret. But my wife got worse and worse. Finally she was taken away to a hospital. She died a year later and, as you can understand, it was a merciful release. But I never forgave those who had deceived me."

Now he spoke bitterly, and Lencia said:

"I can understand that. It must have been terrible for you, and you were too young to cope with it."

"Much too young at the time," he said. "I went to Paris and found that a young man could enjoy himself without being afflicted by being tied to one woman. It made me determined I would never marry again."

"I can understand that," Lencia said, "and I am so very sorry for you."

"There is no need for you to be that," the *Duc* replied. "As *Monsieur Mille-Feuilles,* I have enjoyed every moment of the last six years. I am a free man, and that is how I intend to remain."

"Of course," Lencia said, "but one day you will fall in love."

There was a twist to the *Duc*'s mouth as he said:

"Do you really think I have not been in love already?"

"I am quite certain you have not," Lencia said, "or you would not be talking the way you are now. When you do fall in love, as you will one day, you will find it is very different from the amusements in Paris and the fickle women on whom you have tried to rely."

"Now I suppose you are being prophetic, or else clair-voyant," the *Duc* said.

"I am just telling you the truth," Lencia said. "When you do fall in love you will realise that I have told you the truth."

"But suppose it never happens," the *Duc* said.

He did not wait for her to answer, but went on:

"So often I have said to myself: 'This is different, this is going to be something I have never felt before.' But always the end comes in the same way, and to put it frankly—I am bored."

"That is because you were not really in love." Lencia said.

She was thinking how her Father had fallen in love with her Mother, how happy they had been all through the years they had been together.

"I think," she said slowly, "that one falls in love when one meets what the Greeks called 'the other half of one-self.' Then there is no doubt that this is the one person in the world that you have been seeking."

"Is that what you found?" the *Duc* enquired.

Without thinking, because she was concentrating on him and not on herself, Lencia told the truth.

"No," she said, "but I hope and pray that will happen to me, and I feel sure that one day it will."

It was only then she realised what she had said and rose to her feet.

"But we were talking about you," she said, "and that is what is important. So promise me you will go on seeking, just as Jason sought the Golden Fleece. All men in their hearts want to follow a star."

She did not know why those words came to her lips, but they did.

Then she moved across the room to stand at the balcony, looking out over the beauty of the surrounding country.

It was some seconds before the *Duc* joined her, and then he said:

"Now I find you more mysterious and even more difficult to understand than you were before."

"I am not important," Lencia said. "I am just a ship that passes in the night. What you have to think about is yourself and your own future."

"I have done that for quite some time," the *Duc* said. "Then another leaf comes fluttering at my feet and once again I am optimistic."

"That is what you must continue to be," Lencia said, "because, as I promised you, one day your dreams will come true."

The *Duc* was about to reply, when Alice and Pierre came back into the room.

"We have been right up to the roof," Alice said, "and I am sure I saw a wild boar move among the trees."

"Well, do not go too near it," the *Duc* warned her. "They can be very fierce, especially when there are a number of them together."

"I would be far too frightened to go into the woods at

night," Alice said. "Even at home they are rather creepy after the sun has gone down. You can hear the rabbits in the undergrowth and the deer suddenly move when one least expects it."

"Much better to stay indoors and look for the ghosts," Pierre said.

"We do not have ghosts in our—" Alice stopped.

She was just about to say "Castle," when she caught her sister's eye.

After a second's pause, Alice said rather lamely: "House."

"Well, there are lots of them in Uncle Valaire's *Château*," Pierre said, "so you had better be careful that you do not run into one when you least expect it. You might see one staring down at you when you are lying in bed."

"Now you are frightening me," Alice cried.

"Pay no attention to him," the *Duc* said. "I will not have all this nonsense about ghosts for the simple reason that some women are really frightened by them."

"I expect it is when they hear people tramping about the passages," Pierre said.

Now he was looking at his Uncle in a provocative manner.

"If you are going to be impertinent," the *Duc* said, "I shall send you away tomorrow or forbid you to ride my horses."

"No! no!" Pierre cried, "I apologise."

Now he was speaking theatrically so that they all had to laugh.

"I am sure that would be the worst punishment of all," Lencia said, "if you locked up your horses and just went riding yourself."

"It was a punishment that I suffered as a small boy,"

the *Duc* said, "and one which I shall certainly administer to Pierre if he gets too cheeky."

"I promise I shall speak of you only in the kindest and most adulatory manner," Pierre retorted. "You cannot condemn me to run round the *Château* saying: 'A horse, a horse, my Kingdom for a horse!' "

"I am sure he would not be so cruel," Alice said, "when he has been so kind as to bring me here. And please, can I see more of Chaumont?"

The *Duc* looked at his watch.

"I think we should now go back to luncheon," he said. "I will take you a different way in case we meet any unpleasant characters, who in my opinion are far more trouble than ghosts."

They all knew he was speaking of the *Comte* de Pontlevoy.

Lencia thought it would be a great mistake to meet him and give him the opportunity of being as disagreeable as he had been before.

They left the Castle by one of the doors to which only the *Duc* had a key, and found the carriage without further incident.

They drove back to the *Château*, where there was a delicious luncheon waiting for them.

It was quite late before they left the Dining-Room.

"What I would like now," Pierre announced, "is a game of tennis. Will you play with me, Uncle Valaire?"

"What about our guests?" the *Duc* enquired.

"We both play tennis," Lencia said, "and I hope we are good enough for you."

"Go and find some comfortable shoes," the *Duc* said, "and we shall soon find out how good you are."

As they ran up the stairs, Alice said:

"You are very good, Lencia."

"And you have improved a great deal in the last year," Lencia said. "Anyway, it is good exercise, and if we get in their way, it is just their own fault."

"They are so nice," Alice said, "and I was so glad today that I was not there with that *Comte*. He was trying to be very rude to the *Duc*. What did he mean by calling him *Monsieur Mille-Feuilles?*"

"I expect it is just a French way of being rude," Lencia replied.

They found the two men were very good at tennis, but managed to keep their end up.

Lencia served unusually well for a woman because she had had lessons.

When they were all exhausted they lay under the trees.

The *Duc* ordered a delicious fruit cup to be brought out for them, which was very refreshing.

"We certainly did not expect all this to happen when we left England," Alice remarked, "and I cannot help wondering what we will do next."

"I will tell you what we will do after dinner," Pierre said. "We will play Uncle Valaire's new Phonograph and I will dance with you, unless you are very heavy on your feet."

"Now you are being insulting," Alice said, "I am longing to see a Phonograph, as I have never seen one."

"If you lived with my Uncle," Pierre replied, "you would realise he always has the very latest gadgets."

Lencia looked at the *Duc*.

"Is that true?" she asked.

"I try," he said. "It bores me to read about things in the newspapers and not be able to utilise them for myself."

"I have read about the Phonograph," Lencia said.

"Actually Pierre does not realise that at the moment I have just bought a Berliner Gramophone."

"That is even more exciting," Lencia exclaimed.

"I think it is one of the novelties which will be improved a great deal in the coming years," the *Duc* said. "Tomorrow I want to show you another new acquisition which I have been working on for sometime."

"What is that?" Lencia enquired.

"It is a motor-boat which I have built so that it can navigate the Loire which, as perhaps you know, is very shallow."

"That will be exciting," Lencia said.

Then in a low voice she added:

"You are so kind to have us here. It has made a wonderful holiday for my sister."

"And I hope for you," the *Duc* said

"I am thrilled by everything I see and more happy to be here than I can put into words."

"That is what I want you to say," the *Duc* answered. "For my part it has given me a great deal of pleasure to have you as my guests. You so much enhance the beauty of the *Château* which I have always thought in itself is very lovely."

Once again he was complimenting her and Lencia managed to smile and not blush.

"How long have you been out of mourning?" the *Duc* asked.

Thinking of her Mother and forgetting he was talking about her mythical husband, Lencia said:

"The twelve months finished a month ago, so we need no longer wear black."

"I think with your hair and your skin," the *Duc* said meditatively, "that black would make you look somewhat theatrical but, of course, no less lovely."

"I prefer pale colours," Lencia said, "and now that I

can go to Balls, I shall have some very pretty gowns in pale blue and perhaps pink."

"In which you will look like a rosebud," the *Duc* said. "Or should I say a rose in bloom?"

"The latter is, of course, more correct," Lencia said quickly.

"I am not at all certain that is right," the *Duc* rejoined. "There is something very young about you. In fact, I find it difficult to think that you are much more than twenty."

Lencia gave an affected little laugh.

"Now you are certainly paying me compliments. I suppose no woman likes to think she looks her real age."

"It depends how old she is," the *Duc* said. "But I am telling you there is something very young about you, and I feel you are hardly any older than Alice."

Lencia laughed again.

"I suppose we would all like to put back the clock. But think, if I were a *débutante*, how bored you would be talking to me."

"Why should you think that?" the *Duc* asked.

"Because I have always been told that dashing young Gentlemen like yourself find *débutantes* very boring, and, of course, they are frightened they will be dragged up the aisle, which is the ambition of every *débutante*'s Mother."

Perhaps it was something she should not have said after their conversation that morning.

The *Duc*, however, replied:

"Perhaps you are right. I suppose that is the English point of view, but it does not trouble a Frenchman so much."

"You mean because they have arranged marriages?" Lencia said.

"That is quick of you," he said approvingly. "A man

does not have to look for his first wife, his parents do it for him."

"I think it is a horrible idea," Lencia said, "and look what happened to you."

"Something like that happens once in a million times," the *Duc* said. "All the same, it is right that blue blood should go to blue blood. As you know, the French are very proud about their ancestry and very fussy that it should not be soiled in any way by an unfortunate liaison."

"It is the same with Royalty," Lencia said. "That is, of course, why we forgive Kings like Charles II and, as you pointed out this morning, our Prince of Wales looking for amusements outside their Palaces."

"With often disastrous results," the *Duc* said. "I think your idea of meeting someone with whom one falls madly and crazily but permanently in love is far more satisfactory, but unfortunately it very seldom happens."

"One day it will happen to you," Lencia said. "As I told you this morning, you are not to feel that your life is not as perfect as you want it to be. You are still young, and I am quite certain your Guardian Angel in Heaven is looking after you and will bring the right person to you."

She spoke with a sincerity which was somehow rather touching.

The *Duc* put out his hand and laid it over hers.

"This is the first time," he said, "that anyone has said that to me, and I am very grateful."

Lencia smiled at him.

Then she was aware that because his hand was touching hers, a little thrill ran through her.

She could not explain it to herself.

She only knew it was something she had never felt before.

chapter five

THAT evening after dinner Pierre and Alice danced to the Gramophone.

The *Duc*, however, said he did not have the right records.

"I am making plans for tomorrow," he said just before they went off to bed. "And I have got an idea which I think you will all enjoy."

They looked at him attentively, and he went on:

"First of all we will not ride before breakfast, which is rather tiring, but in the morning. Then, after luncheon, I want to show you my motor-boat, which I think is unique."

"I would love that," Lencia said.

"I am afraid Alice may be a little disappointed," the *Duc* continued, "but I promise her that the following day we will visit at least three *Châteaux*, which will keep her happy for a long time."

"Three will be exciting," Alice said, "even though tomorrow will be a bit of a wasted day."

They all laughed at her for saying this, and the *Duc* said:

"Perhaps, Alice, you will forgive me when I tell you that tomorrow night I have arranged for someone to come and play real music for us to dance to."

Alice clasped her hands together.

"A Ball all of our very own," she exclaimed.

"Exactly," the *Duc* said. "Just a little Ball for you and me, and we hope the rest of the party will enjoy it."

Alice moved impulsively to him and without thinking laid her cheek against his shoulder.

"You are so kind," she said, "I do not know how to thank you."

"Thank me by both of you looking very beautiful tomorrow night," the *Duc* said.

When they went up to bed Alice was talking excitedly about being able to dance to what the *Duc* had called real music.

She had forgotten that she would miss her beloved Castles for one day.

Lencia found it rather pleasant to rise later the next morning.

She went down to breakfast in her riding-habit.

"There is a lot of my Estate that I want to show you," the *Duc* said when they rose from the table. "I think you will find it particularly lovely, and if Alice is lucky, she should see a wild boar."

They set off for quite a long ride.

Lencia thought the *Duc* had underestimated the beauty of their surroundings, which she found breathtaking.

The woods, the pasture land, and the views were lovelier than any countryside she had ever seen before or imagined.

"This is fairyland," she said to the *Duc*, "and I think you are very lucky to live in it."

"That is what I think myself," he said, "and why I try to make my Castle as perfect as it is possible for it to be."

"I have been looking at your treasures," Lencia said, "and I can understand how much they mean to you."

"Most of them are beautiful, like you," he said, "and I should mind losing them just as any man who owned you would be desperate if he lost you."

He was flirting with her again.

At the same time, Lencia felt that he spoke with a sincerity which was difficult to ignore.

She tried to change the subject, but the *Duc* said:

"I was wondering if there is anything you do not do well: You ride better than any woman I have ever seen, you play tennis very well for a member of your sex, and, of course, you make every man's heart turn a somersault as soon as he sees you."

Lencia just smiled, and he went on:

"What I am longing to know is what makes your heart throb quicker, and why your marriage was not a success."

"Who said it was not a success?" Lencia enquired.

"You told me you had not found the perfect love, which you promised I would find one day. So after you married you were obviously disappointed."

"I do not want to talk about it," Lencia said quickly.

She pressed her horse forward, and the *Duc* said:

"You cannot go on running away, and you know as well as I do, Lencia, I am intensely curious about you."

She had noticed that he used her Christian name last night, but thought it would be a mistake to challenge it.

Instead, she said:

"If you knew all there is to know, you would be bored, and therefore, *Monsieur Mille-Feuilles*, I only hope I can keep you guessing."

She was speaking lightly because she felt it was the only way she could answer him.

To her surprise, the *Duc* said seriously:

"Do you mean that? Are you really eager to keep me where I am at the moment—at your feet?"

Lencia turned her head away.

Despite her resolution not to be moved by him, she could not help feeling a little tremor run through her.

Then she told herself he was a Frenchman and she must not believe anything he said to her.

"I am waiting for an answer," the *Duc* said after a short silence.

"Perhaps it is good for you to wait," Lencia said. "I am sure all those lovely *fleurs* you met in Paris fell into your arms the moment you appeared."

"Now you are just guessing," the *Duc* said. "Although I like a puzzle, I want to be confident I can solve it in the last chapter."

"And if you fail?" Lencia asked.

"Then like the ghost in the Castle, you will haunt me."

Lencia thought that was possible.

When they went back to England without his knowing who she was, there would be no chance of their ever seeing each other again.

"The answer to what you are thinking," the *Duc* said, "is that if you leave me in ignorance, I shall always feel that by sheer stupidity I have lost something irreplaceable."

"No-one could accuse you of that," Lencia answered. "At the same time, the answer to some questions are rather like the stars, out of reach."

She moved forward before the *Duc* could reply.

It was, she told herself, getting difficult to go on keeping him in ignorance of who they were and where they came from.

When they returned for luncheon, Pierre talked about the motor-boat.

"It is entirely due to Uncle Valaire," he said proudly, "that the barges moving on the Loire and the canals round here are now using Priestman engines. It makes them go faster and in that way saves a lot of money."

"How clever of you," Lencia exclaimed. "I am sure no-one else has ever thought of having engines in barges."

"On the contrary, they tried it in England first," the *Duc* replied. "But it was a Keystone-engine craft, ahead of its time, having high-tension ignition."

As he finished speaking, he laughed.

"You will not understand what I am saying, but I am quite prepared to take the credit for having introduced the Priestman engines to France, which have proved a great success."

"And that, I suppose, is the engine your motor-boat has," Lencia said a little tentatively.

"You are quite right," the *Duc* replied, "and I had to have something very simple to use on the Loire because it is so shallow, flowing between sand-banks on either side. If you move from the centre of the River, you get into trouble unless your boat is of very shallow draught."

"I understand," Lencia said, "I am longing to see your motor-boat."

"It really is unique," Pierre said, "until that ghastly *Comte* of Alice's copied Uncle Valaire."

"He is not my *Comte*," Alice protested. "I think he is horrible and I hope we do not see him again."

"Did he really copy your motor-boat?" Lencia enquired.

"He did, as he has copied so many other ideas of mine," the *Duc* said, "but there is nothing I can do about it."

"The *Comte* uses his boat for different purposes than Uncle Valaire uses his," Pierre announced. "He has built a sort of hood over it like one has on a Chaise, so that he can sit inside it with a girl and not be seen."

"Stop talking about him," the *Duc* commanded, "and let us go down to the River. The carriage is waiting."

They got into the carriage and drove down to the Loire.

Its course was almost straight where it flowed through the *Duc*'s land.

They could see it glittering away into the far distance towards Orleans.

Because the River was low, the sand-banks were visible on either side of it.

Lencia could understand how important it was to have a boat which would not go aground.

The *Duc* was expected, and the motor-boat was ready outside the Boathouse.

As it was the first one she had ever seen, Lencia was thrilled at the sight of it.

It was, in fact, smaller than she had expected.

There were two seats in front and two behind.

They inspected it and were about to get into it, when the *Duc* said to Lencia:

"I want to show you the inside of the Boathouse. I have invented also a special way of lifting up the boat so that the hull can be cleaned easily underneath after it has got a lot of sand sticking to it. It is a lift which I do not think anyone else has thought of so far."

"I would love to see it," Lencia said.

They went into the Boathouse while Pierre and Alice walked a little way along the side of the River.

He was throwing stones and showing her how by sleight of hand he could make them jump along the surface.

"Oh! I must try that," Alice said, and went down to the edge of the bank.

The lift was as the *Duc* had described it.

His man who was in charge of the boat and the Boat-house demonstrated how the machine worked to raise the boat.

"I do think that was clever of you," Lencia said, "and of course I can understand that when the water is very low, it is impossible for the hull not to get clogged with sand."

"I sometimes wish I lived on a deeper River," the *Duc* admitted, "but at the same time, I love the Loire. It has a beauty of its own, and if it gives us problems, then obviously one has to solve them."

"As you do most effectively," Lencia said.

He smiled at her, then suddenly Pierre burst into the Boathouse.

"Uncle Valaire! Uncle Valaire!" he cried. "The *Comte* has kidnapped Alice!"

"What do you mean?" the *Duc* asked sharply.

"He came along in his boat, saw us, and asked Alice if he could give her a ride. Though she refused, he threw a rope ashore and made fast to a stake on the river-bank. When she told him again she did not want to go with him, he said:

'Very well. Pierre, loosen the rope for me, otherwise I cannot move away.' "

Pierre, who was breathless, paused before he said:

"While I went to do so, the *Comte* lifted Alice into the boat, released the rope, and drove off!"

"How awful! How dreadful!" Lencia cried.

The *Duc* walked towards the door.

"Quickly," he said, "I shall be able to overtake him if we hurry."

Lencia and Pierre both ran and got into the motor-boat.

Pierre sat behind and Lencia next to the *Duc*.

His man released the ropes holding it and the *Duc* started up the engine.

With a roar they began moving up the River.

"Do you know where . . . he has . . . gone?" Lencia asked, having to raise her voice above the noise of the engine.

"I imagine the Devil will take her to his *Château*," the *Duc* replied, "which is a little way up the River beyond Chaumont."

The *Duc* spoke sharply, and there was a grim look in his eyes which told Lencia that he was vey angry.

She guessed it was not entirely because he wanted Alice that the *Comte* had carried her away so outrageously.

He hated the *Duc* and wanted to hurt him in any way he could.

At the same time, she was very worried about Alice, knowing how frightened she would be.

"Why," she asked herself, "did we ever come on this trip? If we had stayed at home, there would have been no unpleasant *Comte* to behave in such an appalling way."

But she could not help thinking that there would also have been no kind and charming *Duc*.

Then she forced herself to think only of Alice.

If the *Comte* was alone in his motor-boat, he could hardly frighten her by trying to kiss her.

Anything like that was out of the question while he was manipulating the boat.

It was therefore essential that the *Duc* should overtake him before he reached his own *Château*.

"How fast can you go?" she asked nervously.

"Faster than the *Comte* can manage in his boat," the *Duc* replied. "He thought he was copying me exactly, but I found out from Priestman that he had squeezed down the price and they had not given him exactly the same horse-power as they had given me."

Lencia looked ahead but could not see any sign of the *Comte*'s boat.

The *Duc* was in the centre of the River, driving his engine to the utmost of its power.

There were, however, three people in his boat and only two in the *Comte*'s.

What was more, the *Comte* was shorter and lighter than the *Duc*.

Pierre, who was a strongly built young man, must, Lencia thought, weigh a great deal.

She clasped her hands together and prayed.

"Please God, let us overtake him, please God, please," she prayed fervently.

Then, as the *Duc* glanced at her, she knew he was aware what she was doing.

"Do not worry," he said, "we will save her all right. I only hope I can prevent myself from killing that man, which is something I have wanted to do for a long time."

"I feel the same," Lencia said, "but please be careful. It would cause a terrible scandal if you did kill him."

She was thinking that because the *Duc* had such a famous name, a fight between the two men would undoubtedly be reported in the newspapers, and there would be questions as to who were accompanying them.

As they had English names, false or otherwise, the English papers might take up the story.

It could happen.

If then it was discovered who Lady Winterton and Miss Austin were, she could not imagine what would be said by their relations and friends.

"Please, please go quicker," she said to the *Duc*.

Behind them Pierre gave a shout.

"There they are!" he said. "I can see them quite clearly."

Lencia could now see them too.

A small motor-boat was moving up the centre of the River.

Now the *Duc* was pushing his boat as hard as he could and gradually they drew nearer and nearer to the *Comte*.

They could see his head above the cover he had placed over the back seats of his motor-boat.

Lencia wondered whether Alice was inside or sitting beside him.

Whichever it was, there was no sign of her.

The *Comte* was now aware they were overtaking him.

A few minutes later they were level with him.

Now, to Lencia's surprise, the *Duc* was bumping his boat heavily against the *Comte's*.

At the first bump the *Comte* shouted:

"Get off, keep away from me!"

Again the *Duc* moved in, banging against the side of the *Comte's* boat so that it was forced a foot or so over to the left.

Again the *Comte* screamed at them.

It was, however, difficult to hear what he was saying above the noise of the engines.

Then, as Lencia waited for the next impact, she understood what the *Duc* was doing.

He was forcing the *Comte* away from the centre of the River towards the sand-banks.

In some places the sand-banks were below the surface of the water, but they were still there.

They made the River impassable to any craft that did not keep to the centre of it.

Bang—bang—and bang again.

This time the *Comte*'s boat ran onto a sand-bank and could not move any further forward.

The *Duc* gave it another bang to make quite certain it was stuck fast.

As the *Comte* stood up shouting and swearing, Lencia bent over to look for Alice.

She was on the seat at the back of the boat and was obviously terrified by what was happening.

It was then that Pierre acted.

The *Comte*, standing up in his boat, was so enraged that his face was crimson.

He was leaning forward to try and make himself heard above the roar of the engines.

Before the *Comte* could realise what was happening, Pierre had jumped onto his boat and pushed him over the side into the River.

He then pulled Alice up from the back seat and held her in his arms.

As the *Duc* steadied his boat, Pierre lifted her into it.

There was just one precarious moment before he joined her, but he managed to spring over the gap between the boats.

The *Duc* turned his boat round slowly and carefully so that they could go back the way they had come.

As he did so, Lencia saw the *Comte* was standing by his now-useless boat up to his waist in water.

He was shaking his fist at them.

He was obviously cursing them, but fortunately they could not hear what he was saying.

As the *Duc* started off down the River, Lencia turned round to ask Alice:

"Are you all right, Darling? He has not hurt you?"

Alice had Pierre's arms around her and raised her head from his shoulder to say:

"I am all right, but I was very . . . very . . . frightened."

"Of course you were," Pierre said, "but you must have known that Uncle Valaire would save you."

"I . . . prayed that . . . you would . . . come," Alice said, "but I could . . . not see . . . and when I . . . begged the *Comte* to . . . stop he . . . did not hear . . . me."

"He did not want to," Pierre said. "You are not the first girl he has kidnapped like this."

"I will speak to the Head of Police about him," the *Duc* said grimly. "This sort of behaviour cannot go on."

"But . . . you saved . . . me," Alice said, "and thank . . . you very . . . much. I felt . . . sure you . . . would do . . . so but I . . . could not help being . . . frightened. He is such a . . . nasty man."

"Well, it is going to take him some time to get his motor-boat off that sand-bank," Pierre said, "and I hope he catches a cold."

"It was clever of you to throw him overboard," the *Duc* said. "At the same time, if he had hit his head and knocked himself out, we would have had to rescue him."

"Personally I would gladly have let him drown," Pierre said.

"That would have been asking too much of fate," the *Duc* said, "but I think for the moment he has learned his lesson. No man likes being made to look a fool."

They took the motor-boat back to the Boathouse.

They started to walk back across some rough ground to where the carriage was waiting.

As they did so, a little boy came running through the trees.

He was chasing a rabbit which disappeared into the undergrowth in front of him.

As it did, the boy tripped over a large stone and fell.

Before anyone else could move, the *Duc* reached him and picked him up.

The small boy had given a scream and now he was crying.

"You must be very brave," the *Duc* said. "You have not hurt yourself, and the little rabbit has gone away."

The boy's tears stopped.

Because the *Duc* was holding him high in his arms, he looked at him with interest.

"I wanted to catch that rabbit," he said.

"I think it would have been too quick for you," the *Duc* answered. "But I tell you what you can do: you can go and buy yourself some sweets at the shop and I will give you the money to do so."

The child was all smiles and at that moment his Mother appeared.

She was carrying a baby in her arms, and as she hurried towards them, Lencia said to her:

"It is all right. Your son tripped and fell down, but he is not hurt."

"I think he has scratched his knee," the *Duc* said. "He fell against a stone, and it is bleeding a little."

"I will soon stop it, *Monsieur*," the Mother said.

The *Duc* sat down on a fallen tree trunk and put the boy on his knee.

Now Lencia could see it was not a bad cut.

"Let me hold the baby," she said to the Mother.

The woman handed her the small baby and brought a clean handkerchief out of her pocket.

The baby must have been no more than three weeks old.

It was a pretty child, with just a few dark hairs on its head and large dark eyes.

Its shawl was spotlessly clean.

Lencia was certain that the Mother looked after both her children well.

The woman now hurried towards the *Duc*, who was showing a silver coin to the little boy.

When she saw who he was, she curtsied and said:

"I'm sorry that my son has inconvenienced you, *Monsieur le Duc*."

"I think he has inconvenienced himself," the *Duc* replied. "He was chasing a rabbit, and you will never stop a small boy doing that."

The woman quickly wiped the trickles of blood from the boy's knee.

The *Duc* put him down on the ground.

"What is his name?" he asked.

There was a little pause and then the woman said:

"I hope, *Monsieur*, you'll not think it impertinent, but we christened him after you."

"I am very honoured," the *Duc* said, "I hope that Valaire will grow up to be a strong young man like my nephew. Does your husband work for me?"

"Yes, *Monsieur*, he is one of the woodmen."

"Then tell him I am very pleased that his son is interested in the woods already, and of course there will be a place for him in them when he grows up."

"Thank you, *Monsieur*, thank you," the woman said.

The *Duc* rose from the tree trunk on which he had been sitting.

He handed the small boy the piece of silver he had been showing him and said:

"This is for you to buy some sweets."

He took another coin from his pocket which Lencia thought was a gold Louis.

"And this," he said, "is to buy a present for your Mother. You must always, as you grow older, give your Mother presents, because she looks after you."

"I'll do that," the small boy said.

The *Duc* put his hand on the boy's head, and then he said:

"When you do manage to catch a rabbit, tell your Father to tell me about it."

"Yes, *Monsieur*," the small boy replied.

He was, however, looking at the coins with delight.

His Mother came back, and Lencia said:

"This is a beautiful baby. Is it a boy or a girl?"

"A girl, *Madame*," the woman said.

"Have you had her christened yet?" the *Duc* asked.

"She's being christened next Sunday, *Monsieur*."

"Then I will give her one of her names," the *Duc* said. "Do not forget it. It is Lencia."

"That's a very pretty name, *Monsieur le Duc*, and I'll not forget," the woman said.

She took the baby from Lencia and managed to curtsy to the *Duc*.

He bade her good-day and, taking Lencia by the arm, helped her up the last steps which led onto the road.

"Now we have two people bearing our names," he said, "and I wonder what their lives will be like."

"If they are as fortunate as we are, very, very happy," Lencia said.

"How can you be sure that applies to us?" the *Duc* enquired.

There was no time to answer him, as the carriage drew up beside them.

Alice and Pierre had been waiting for them on the road, and they drove back to the *Château*.

Lencia noticed that the *Duc* made himself very pleasant to Alice.

It was as if he was re-assuring her after being upset and frightened.

'He is very kind,' Lencia thought.

She was also touched by the way he had treated the small son of one of his woodmen.

'I am sure all the people on his Estate adore him,' she thought.

They had tea and then the *Duc* and Pierre said they were going to play Billiards.

It gave Lencia an opportunity to rest before dinner.

She had, in fact, although she told herself it was stupid, been considerably upset by what had happened to Alice.

She thought too that Alice looked pale.

"Have a little sleep," she said, "then we will be sparkling at dinner. Do not forget the *Duc* has engaged someone to play for us so that we can dance afterwards. It is to be in the Music-Room, because the Ballroom is too big."

"It will be very exciting to dance with Pierre," Alice said. "Even if it is not a real Ball, at least we shall not have any competition."

Lencia smiled.

"And we are bound to have a partner for every dance," she answered.

Alice laughed, and then she said:

"Wear Mama's best dress tonight. You may not get another chance, and it is so pretty."

Lencia had not thought of it.

Now it seemed to her a sensible thing to do, having brought it all the way to France.

When she put it on, she knew it was extremely becoming.

Yet because it was made of such soft material and had quite a low *décolleté*, it made her appear very young.

She wore the diamond necklace and the ear-rings which went with it.

"You look wonderful!" Alice exclaimed when she came into her bedroom. "Pierre has sent me up some flowers which the Maid has arranged in my hair."

They made Alice look very pretty.

It gave a finishing touch to her white gown in which she hoped, if she was allowed to, to come to one of the *débutante* dances that were to be given for her sister.

"No-one can say we are not dressed in our best," Lencia said as they walked downstairs. "I only hope the two Gentlemen waiting for us appreciate the effort we have made on their behalf."

"I am sure they will," Alice said. "It is so wonderful to be here, dancing with Pierre, when I might have been . . ."

"Do not think about it," Lencia said sharply, knowing what Alice was about to say. "You know very well we should have rescued you even if he had taken you as far as his *Château*."

"Pierre was very brave to push him in the River and lift me into the *Duc's* boat," Alice said, as if she was re-living it.

Lencia gave a little sigh.

If Alice were to fall in love with Pierre, it would make things even more complicated than they were already.

"I think," she told herself, "we shall soon have to go home."

At the same time, she knew she wanted to stay.

She had never enjoyed anything so much as being in this fabulous Castle with the *Duc*.

He paid her unbelievable compliments, but there was no-one to criticise or say unkind things.

"It is too good to last," Lencia said to herself.

But she was smiling and her eyes were shining as she went into the Drawing-Room, where the men were waiting.

After dinner was finished, they went into the Music-Room.

It was decorated with flowers and was one of the prettiest rooms Lencia had ever seen.

Seated at the piano, which was on a small dais at the far end of the room, was a young man.

She had somehow expected an older musician or perhaps a woman.

The young man seemed about the same age as Pierre.

He wore his hair rather too long, obviously as a sign of his artistic ability.

When he started to play the piano, Lencia knew he was an outstanding musician.

He was playing a dreamy waltz, one written by Richard Strauss, who had become popular not only in Europe but also in England.

"This is the moment I have been looking forward to," the *Duc* said.

He put his arm around Lencia's waist.

As he took her hand in his, she felt a little thrill run through her.

She told herself it was just because she was dancing with a handsome young man.

At the same time, she was aware it was the same feeling she had felt last night when the *Duc* touched her hand.

He swung her round on the polished floor.

He was an excellent dancer, just as he excelled both as a horseman and a tennis-player.

They danced in silence.

Yet there seemed to Lencia to be something magical about the music, the flower-scented room and, of course, the closeness of the *Duc*.

"It is because he is so overwhelmingly important," she told herself.

But she knew that what she was feeling was due to being close to him.

His hand was holding hers, and it was something very personal and very intimate.

They danced for a long time.

The young man at the piano kept changing from tune to tune.

He always chose those which were romantic and exciting.

The *Duc* finally stopped at the open window.

They looked out into the garden, where the great fountain was playing in the moonlight.

"I knew you would be as light as thistledown," the *Duc* said quitely, "and that we would move together as if we were one person. Did you feel that?"

"You are a very good dancer," Lencia said.

"You have not answered my question," he replied.

She looked up at him, and when their eyes met, it was difficult to look away.

Then, as the music changed, the *Duc* drew her back

into the room.

Once again they were moving round the floor.

He was right: they moved as if they were one person, joined not only by their bodies but by their minds.

It was not very late when the *Duc* thanked the pianist and sent him away.

"I want to go on dancing," Alice complained.

"We have all had a long day and there will doubtless be another long one tomorrow," the *Duc* said, "so I think we should go to bed."

"I am sure you are right," Lencia said. "It is stupid to get over-tired, and nothing is more tiring than dramas."

She saw Alice shiver as she thought of the *Comte*, and hurried her up to her room.

"It has been a traumatic day," she said. "Go to sleep, Dearest, and there is always tomorrow. Remember, the *Duc* has promised to take you to three different Castles."

"I am looking forward to that," Alice said.

She put her arms round her sister's neck and said:

"It is so lovely being here. I want to stay for ever and ever."

"It is no use, we shall soon have to go home," Lencia replied. "We cannot risk Papa and Stepmama arriving back and finding we are missing."

Alice sighed.

"No, of course not. But how can we ever come here again if the *Duc* does not know where to find us?"

"Perhaps we will tell him, and perhaps we will not," Lencia said. "I have not yet made up my mind."

Then she said quickly:

"Yes, I have! He must never, never know who we are. You do understand?"

"I suppose so," Alice said, "but I want to see Pierre again."

"In a year or so it may be possible for you to meet him in London," Lencia said.

She knew her sister was pouting and looking disappointed.

She kissed her goodnight and went to her own room.

As she took off her Mother's dress she could hear the *Duc* saying:

"I have never seen you dressed like that before. You look entrancing, as a hundred men must have told you."

Lencia shook her head, and he said:

"Where you live the men must be blind, deaf, and dumb."

"In England," Lencia said, "salmon, grouse, and pheasants are so much more attractive."

The *Duc* laughed as she had intended him to do.

Then once again he was serious and said:

"You bewilder me, but at the same time I am bewitched. What do you intend to do about it, Lencia?"

"What can I do?" she answered.

The *Duc* did not reply.

Alice and Pierre joined them and there was no longer a private conversation.

"How can he say such things and not mean them?" Lencia asked herself as she undressed.

She brushed her hair as her Mother had always told her to do.

She put out the lights except for two beside her bed.

It was a very large bed hung with both muslin and satin curtains.

It had a canopy of gilded cupids.

There were also cupids on the painted ceiling and surrounding the mirror on the dressing table.

'It is a room made for love,' Lencia thought.

Then she blushed because it seemed to be the wrong thing for her to be thinking.

She said her prayers, and before putting out the lights, she looked around to have a last impression of the beautiful room which she knew she would never forget.

Then the door at the far end opened.

It was a door which led into a little *boudoir* which she had hardly used because there had been no reason to do so.

She thought it was Alice for some reason coming to her.

Then, to her surprise, she saw it was the *Duc*.

chapter six

LENCIA stared at the *Duc* in astonishment.

Then, as he crossed the room, she asked:

"What has . . . happened? Why are you . . . here?"

"I have come to finish our conversation," the *Duc* replied.

"But you should not come into my bedroom," Lencia protested. "Please go . . . away."

The *Duc* smiled, and as he came nearer he looked at her.

He thought he had never seen her look so lovely.

Her fair hair was falling over her shoulders.

She was wearing one of her Mother's diaphanous night-gowns which she had thought would impress the Housemaids.

It revealed the curves of her breasts.

Then, as she saw the *Duc* looking at her, she pulled up the sheet to cover them.

"You must . . . go . . . away," she said sternly, but her voice trembled a little.

The *Duc* sat down on the side of the bed.

"Now, listen, Lencia," he said. "You cannot go on mourning for a man whom you have admitted you did not really love. I think since you have been here, you and I have realised that we have so much in common that if we were a little closer still, it would make us both very happy."

Lencia drew in her breath.

She knew exactly what he was saying to her.

She was shocked, but knew it was her own fault.

"Please go . . . away," she said quickly, "and we will talk . . . about it . . . tomorrow."

"Why not now?" the *Duc* asked. "I want to tell you how lovely you are, and how much I want you."

He paused for a moment, and then he went on:

"God knows I have been patient enough in respecting your bereavement. I believed rather foolishly that you had been very much in love with your husband."

It was difficult for Lencia to know what to reply.

She knew only that the *Duc* was sitting on her bed, looking at her.

He was wearing a long robe which was very much the same as her Father wore.

Because she was frightened, not of him, but of her feelings towards him, she said again:

"Please . . . please go away now, and . . . perhaps we will think . . . about . . . it."

"What have we got to think about?" the *Duc* asked. "Except that you are the most beautiful person I have ever seen and I want you unbearably."

He gave a little smile before he added:

"I cannot tell you how many hours I have lain awake

at night, thinking of you and wanting to come here and tell you how irresistible I find you. But I thought it was right to wait."

"Of course . . . it was . . . right," Lencia said, "and please you must . . . go on . . . waiting."

"Why must I?" the *Duc* asked. "Tonight when we were dancing together and our steps matched each other's, I know, though you tried to hide it, that you were as thrilled as I was."

He moved a little nearer to her and said:

"Stop playing with me, Lencia, and let us be happy as the Gods intended. We met by chance and found they had in fact been very, very kind."

He bent forward and Lencia thought he was about to kiss her.

She gave a little cry and held him off with both hands.

"No! No!" she cried. "You are . . . not to . . . touch me, you are . . . not to."

"Why?" the *Duc* asked. "You have bewildered me ever since I met you, and still I find you impossible to understand."

He did not touch her, but his face was very near to hers as he said:

"I think, although you will not admit it, that you want me as I want you. Be sensible, Lencia, and let me teach you about love, a love which I am sure no Englishman could give you."

Lencia was still pushing at his chest with both her hands.

Now she said almost angrily:

"Go away . . . you are . . . tempting me to do . . . something which is . . . wrong and which I . . . cannot do."

The *Duc* sat up, and her hands fell away from his chest.

"Wrong?" he asked, "Why should it be wrong? You are free now, and I am free. If we love each other, who is to find anything wrong in that?"

"I cannot . . . explain," Lencia said, "but it would be wrong . . . very wrong and . . . wicked for me to . . . allow you to make . . . love to . . . me."

"I do not understand," the *Duc* said.

"And I . . . cannot tell you . . . the reason," Lencia said. "Please be . . . kind, as you have . . . been so very . . . kind already, and . . . go away and . . . forget me."

"Do you think that is possible?" the *Duc* said.

"It has to be . . . for . . . reasons that I . . . cannot tell you."

There was a little sob in Lencia's voice.

Now there were tears in her eyes as she said:

"There is . . . nothing I can tell you . . . nothing I can say . . . except that . . . you must . . . listen to me and please . . . leave me . . . alone."

The *Duc* seemed to stiffen, and then he said:

"I have never forced myself on a woman who did not want me. If you really mean what you say, then there is nothing I can do, Lencia, but to leave you."

She did not reply, then after a moment he said:

"Tell me this mysterious secret, tell me what you are hiding from me. You cannot leave me in ignorance and then expect me to understand."

"I would tell you . . . if I . . . could," Lencia said. "But it is . . . impossible."

"Nothing is impossible," the *Duc* said. "We are two people attracted to each other, as was intended, I believe, from the beginning of time. As I have just said, I am a free man and you are a free woman, and what could be wrong in our love?"

He waited for a reply, and as she was silent, he said:

"Tell me, Darling, tell me this momentous secret. If it is a problem that needs solving, I am quite certain that it is something I can do."

Now that he was pleading with her, it was even harder to resist him than it had been before.

She was tempted to tell him the truth.

Then she knew he might be shocked and, worse still, might think it was a ruse to trap him into marriage.

If her Father became aware that she was there unchaperoned, he would doubtless tell the *Duc* that he had ruined her reputation.

The only way he could make amends would be to offer her marriage.

It all flashed through Lencia's mind.

Then she said aloud:

"I would . . . tell you if it was . . . possible, but you must . . . believe me when I say . . . that it is . . . absolutely . . . impossible. Therefore I can only . . . beg you to be . . . kind and . . . go away. Please let us . . . forget that . . . this ever . . . happened."

The *Duc* gave a deep sigh.

"Very well, Lencia," he said, "I have no wish to upset you or make you unhappy. But tomorrow perhaps you will change your mind."

The *Duc* rose to his feet.

As he did so, Lencia put out her hand towards him.

"Please do . . . not be . . . angry," she begged. "You have made Alice and me so . . . happy here and we are . . . so grateful to . . . you. I do not . . . want to hurt . . . you."

"This has never happened to me before," he said. "I feel frustrated at being confronted with a problem I cannot solve and a mystery I cannot penetrate."

"But you . . . are not . . . angry?" Lencia asked.

She looked up at him pleadingly, her eyes still glistening a little with tears.

He stood looking down at her, and then unexpectedly he bent forward and kissed her.

It was a very gentle kiss.

As his lips touched her, Lencia felt as if a shaft of sunshine swept through her whole body.

It was so rapturous, so incredible that she could hardly believe it was happening.

Just for a moment the *Duc*'s kiss deepened.

Then he raised his head and stood very still, looking at her.

Then without a word he turned and left the room the way he had come without looking back.

It was only when he had gone that Lencia put her hands up to her face.

The rapture and ecstasy she had felt from his kiss was still there.

Then, when she knew she had lost him, the tears came and she hid her face in her pillow.

* * *

Lencia did not sleep until it was almost dawn.

Then she slept from sheer exhaustion.

She kept turning over and over in her mind what the *Duc* had said to her and what she had said to the *Duc*.

But the end was always the same.

He had left her, and the barrier between them was, she thought, even greater than it had been before.

'I love him,' she thought, 'of course I love him. How could I have been with him all this time and not love everything he says and everything he does?'

Even as she confessed it to herself the temptation was there.

She wanted to listen to what he had suggested, to agree that they were made for each other, and let him love her as he wished to do.

It was then she knew she must go home.

When the Maid came to call her, she was deeply asleep.

As she drowsily opened her eyes, the Maid said:

"Pardon, *Madame*, there is a message here from *Monsieur le Duc*."

Lencia sat up in bed.

On the table there was an envelope addressed to Lady Winterton.

For a moment she just stared at it.

Was it possible, because he was angry with her, that he was asking her to leave the Castle?

Had he no further use for her as a guest after last night?

Her hands were trembling as she opened the envelope.

She drew out the piece of writing-paper inside.

On it was written:

"Beautiful Lencia,

I have just received a message to say that the President of France stayed last night with one of my neighbours.

He is very anxious to see Chaumont this morning and of course I have to show him round.

It means unfortunately that Pierre, who has to go with

*me, and I will have to stay for luncheon. But we will hurry
back as quickly as possible. I have, my lovely Goddess, something very important to discuss with you this evening.*

Yours,
Valaire"

Lencia read the letter through and then read it again.

She knew, as if she were being told, that this was
her opportunity to leave without explanations, without
arguments, and without embarrassing farewells.

She got out of bed and went to her sister's room.

Alice was standing at the window in her night-gown,
looking at the sunshine.

"It is a lovely day for riding," she said.

"Listen, Alice," Lencia said. "We have had an urgent
message from home that we have to leave immediately."

Alice turned round sharply.

"From home?"

"That is what we shall tell the Servants," Lencia said.
"We have to leave, and this is our opportunity to go
without being questioned as to when the *Duc* or Pierre
can meet us again."

As she spoke, she held out the note that the *Duc* had
written to her, and Alice read it.

"I do not want to go," she said. "Surely we can stay a
few more days."

"If we do, it will not make it any easier to say goodbye," Lencia said. "You will just have to think of this as
a lovely dream, something we will always remember,
which will never happen again."

"I want to see Pierre again," Alice protested.

"Perhaps that can be arranged when you are a *débutante*
and if he comes to London. But you know as well as I do

that I cannot confess I am an imposter who has deceived the *Duc* into thinking I am a widow. And if Papa knew what we have done, he would be very, very angry."

Alice gave a little shiver.

"Yes, of course he would, and you are right, Lencia. We had better go home while we have the chance."

"Tell your Maid to pack for you and I will tell mine. There is a train at eleven o'clock at Blois which will take us to Paris, and we can catch the afternoon train to Calais."

"Oh, very well," Alice said, "but it seems to me awfully rude."

"Even ruder," Lencia replied, "when they ask us when they can see us again and we will not give them an address."

Alice must have seen the wisdom of this, because she did not say any more.

Lencia hurried back to her own bedroom.

The Housekeeper was surprised they had to leave in such a hurry.

As one of the Maids started to pack Lencia's clothes, a message was sent to the Stables to provide them with a carriage.

As was usual for the *Duc*'s guests, another Servant was sent to the Station.

He would notify the Stationmaster that they would require a private carriage.

Because the Castle was so beautifully run, there seemed to be no difficulties and everything was arranged smoothly.

Lencia tipped everyone generously.

This she could well afford, not having had to pay a Hotel bill while they were away.

She just had time to write a very short note to the *Duc*.
She did not head it but started off saying:

"*I can only thank you from the bottom of my heart for
your kindness to me and my sister.*

*It has been a joy being your guests and for Alice having
her dreams of Chaumont come true.*

*I am sorry we have to leave so hastily, but we have
received word that we are required at home.*

*This has been a magical moment which I shall never
forget.*

Lencia"

She put it into an envelope and addressed it to the *Duc*,
knowing he would receive it as soon as he returned.

As they drove down the drive, she looked back at the
Castle.

She thought it would always be in her dreams, although
she would never see it again.

Alice was very quiet and hardly spoke until the train
left Blois Station.

They had a last glimpse of the trees which hid the
River and a fleeting sight of some *Châteaux* they had not
visited as they passed them by.

"I shall never forget Pierre," Alice said, "but if he is
not allowed to see me for at least a year, I suppose he
will forget me."

"I am sure you will find a great many other young
men to admire you," Lencia said.

"Do you think," Alice asked, "that you will be able to
forget the *Duc*?"

It was a question to which Lencia knew the answer.

She had, however, no intention of sharing it with her
sister.

"I said to him once," she replied, "that we were 'ships that pass in the night,' and that, Dearest, is what we are. At the same time, ships call at many different ports, which I expect we shall do in our lives."

Alice did not answer.

She was looking out of the window.

Lencia knew by the expression on her face that she was miserable at leaving Pierre behind.

They crossed Paris and found the train to Calais at the *Gare du Nord*.

At last Lencia felt she could relax.

In the carriage she sat with her feet up and her eyes closed.

It was then she allowed herself to think of the wonder and glory of the kiss the *Duc* had given her last night.

She felt as if his lips were still pressed against hers.

She could feel again the shaft of sunshine passing through her body.

The incredible rapture of it seemed to carry her into the sky.

She had never been kissed before.

Yet she was wise enough to know that the kiss the *Duc* had given her was different not only from what she had expected but different from the kisses she would receive from other men.

"How could I be such a fool," she asked herself, "as to fall in love with a Frenchman? He has already loved a thousand women, and will doubtless love a thousand more."

Nevertheless, the wheels of the train kept saying: "I love . . . him, I love . . . him, I love . . . him" over and over again.

She felt the tears come into her eyes and start to trickle down her cheeks.

She hastily wiped them away in case Alice should see them.

Alice was, however, deep in her own thoughts.

Lencia could only pray that her love for Pierre was not something which would spoil her life.

If Alice compared every other man she met in England with the fascinating *Vicomte*, she would be in the same boat as Lencia was.

Lencia remembered reading somewhere that one always pays for experience.

That, she thought, was what she was doing now.

She had been brave enough to take Alice to France in disguise.

Now she was paying the price because she had left her heart behind with a Frenchman.

To him she was just one more pretty "flower" to be left by the wayside. . . .

She found it hard later to remember anything of the journey.

It just seemed to be long hours of hearing the wheels of the train repeating: "I love . . . you, I love . . . you."

It was an uncomfortable Channel crossing, with an extremely rough sea.

A great number of the passengers were sea-sick.

Because it was unpleasant to be below, Lencia and Alice sat on deck.

They wrapped themselves in blankets which a Steward brought them.

It was not particularly cold, but there was a strong wind.

They sat in silence until they reached Dover.

Then there was the train-journey back to London and a welcome from the surprised staff at Armeron House.

They had to explain that they had been staying with

friends, and owing to an unexpected change of plans they now had to break their journey home in London.

"Now we have got to get home," Lencia said, "and the quickest way would be by train."

"Papa always hates the train and drives whenever he can," Alice said.

"It is enjoyable for him because he is driving his own horses," Lencia answered. "Those we have here in London can take us as far as the *Three Kings*, but I cannot see how we can get home from there except in a hired carriage."

"Oh! Let us go by train," Alice urged. "We shall be able to get a carriage of some sort to take us from the station to Armeron. After all, it is only four miles."

Because she was feeling despondent, she did not care how they travelled as long as they got home as quickly as possible.

They spent the night in London, and the servants made them as comfortable as they could at short notice.

They made it very clear to Lencia that they did not like their new mistress.

"We miss your Lady Mother, Miss Lencia," they said one after another. "We all loved her an' things aren't the same now she's not here."

Lencia felt that was something she could say herself.

It was typical of her Stepmother to upset the Servants who had been with them for so many years.

"We're all looking forward, Miss Lencia," the House-keeper said, "now you're out of mourning, to your coming to London for parties and, of course, for your Presentation to Her Majesty."

"I am afraid that has had to be postponed," Lencia said, "because Her Ladyship is taking my place at the first Drawing-Room."

She realised as she spoke how shocked the old House-keeper was at the idea.

It was some consolation to know that she too resented it.

Finally Lencia and Alice set off for the Station.

The Butler escorted them and saw them safely into a locked carriage.

A large hamper of food had been prepared by the cook so that they "need not eat that Restaurant stuff."

When they opened the hamper Alice said:

"If we eat all this, we shall be too fat to get out through the door."

"The Servants in London love us, if no-one else does," Lencia said. "I think in a way they are making more fuss over us just to spite Stepmama."

"They hate her just as I do," Alice said. "It is agony to think we have got to put up with her all through the summer."

Then she looked at her sister and laughed.

"It is a good thing she could not see you the other night in Mama's beautiful dress dancing with a *Duc*. She would have wanted to tear your eyes out!"

"Oh, do be careful, Alice!" Lencia said. "No-one must ever know that happened, and if we talk about it even just together, we might be overheard."

"Well, I want to talk about the wonderful time we had in France," Alice protested. "I want to dance with Pierre and race him up the stairs. Instead of which I have got to listen to Stepmama telling me what a success she has been."

"As soon as we get back we will ride the horses and forget her," Lencia said.

It was, however, more easily said than done.

When she went riding the next morning with Alice,

she kept remembering what fun it had been riding with the *Duc*.

She remembered the compliments he had paid her.

Of course, even to think of him brought back the wonder of his kiss.

It was impossible not to think that very soon he would be kissing someone else in the same way.

"How can I ever love anyone else, having loved him?" Lencia asked herself angrily when she was in bed that night.

In the darkness she felt she could see him all too clearly sitting on her bed and pleading with her.

"Why did I say no? Why did I run away?" she asked herself.

She knew all the answers, but the questions were still there.

Nothing seemed to erase them from her mind.

The second day after they got home they learned that the Earl and their Stepmama had arrived back in London from Sweden.

"They are coming down this afternoon," Lencia said. "Mr. Bentley has instructions to send the carriage to the Station."

"What are we going to say if Papa learns, as he is bound to, that we have been to London?" Alice asked nervously.

"We went up because I had to go to the Dentist," Lencia said. "You know we have always been to the same Dentist, and Papa would not dream of having anyone else treat us."

"Then what happened?" Alice said.

"Then we went to stay with a school-friend of mine whom I will invent, or else use the name of one I have mentioned in a letter when I have written home to Mama and Papa."

"So we stayed in London," Alice questioned, trying to get it all clear.

"We stayed in London with my friend, my teeth were treated by the Dentist, and then we came home."

"I will try not to forget it," Alice said, "but it will be very difficult not to tell Papa what he missed by not going to France with us."

She was only teasing, but Lencia said:

"For Heaven's sake, Alice, we have managed to escape without anyone penetrating our disguise, and we must not push our luck too far. You know how angry Papa would be."

"Egged on by Stepmama," Alice agreed bitterly, "who would be delighted if we were in trouble."

"Well, do not give her the satisfaction of having a genuine cause for complaint," Lencia said.

She had thought their stay over very carefully.

She was very certain her Father would not be suspicious if she and Alice told the same tale.

When the Earl finally arrived home, she realised she need not have worried.

Their Father was looking rather tired and seemed not to have enjoyed himself in Sweden.

But their Stepmother never stopped talking.

She told them how they had been received almost as if they were Royalty, describing in detail the palatial rooms they were given, the huge Dinner Parties they attended.

She went on to describe the Ball, the presents the Prince had received, and the speeches which had been made.

It all took a long time.

Lencia forced herself to sit, looking attentive, as if she were really interested in what her Stepmother was saying.

"We promised to go back next year," the Countess said triumphantly, "and we have also been invited to visit Denmark. That is something I know we shall enjoy."

"What about you, Papa?" Lencia asked.

She realised her Father had not said a word for at least twenty minutes.

"I find it tiring to go gadding about when I want to be at home," he replied. "Tell me about the horses."

Lencia described how well they were.

Fortunately he did not ask if she had been riding every day, but took it for granted.

It did come up a little later that Lencia had had to go to London to see the Dentist.

But almost before she could say anything, the Countess interrupted by interposing.

"That reminds me, I want my bedroom in London redecorated, and the sooner it is done the better."

The Earl looked surprised.

"What is wrong with it, my Dear?" he asked. "It always seemed delightful to me."

"You are so understanding, Dearest," his wife replied, "so you will, I know, appreciate that I want my bedroom to represent me and me alone."

She put out her hand to touch his shoulder as she said:

"Of course I want to look beautiful in it for you. And who is a better judge of beauty than the handsome and very clever Earl of Armeron?"

She was flattering him again, Lencia knew.

Because it was false and insincere, it made her feel sick.

She got up from the chair and walked across the room.

"I meant to tell you, Lencia," her Father said as if he had suddenly thought of it, "that I saw the Lord Chamberlain about your Presentation. He has managed

127

to squeeze you into the last one, which will take place in June."

"Oh, very well, Papa," Lencia said, "but I would rather have been in one earlier."

"The Lord Chamberlain said it was impossible," the Earl replied, "and I am very sorry that we had to change it from the first."

"Perhaps it would be better, Dearest, if Lencia waited another year," the Countess murmured.

"No, of course not," the Earl replied. "Lencia is nineteen. She should have been presented last year if she had not been in mourning."

"I expect she will feel rather out of place with all those *débutantes* of seventeen and eighteen," the Countess said. "But I dare say no-one will really notice that she is much older."

Lencia knew that she was trying to make it difficult for her.

She thought it best not to reply or make any objections.

"What we must have," the Earl said quickly, "is some young parties for Lencia in London, and perhaps it would be wise to give our Ball rather sooner than we intended so that we will be invited to all the other Balls."

"I am looking forward to a Ball," the Countess said. "But we do not want too many young people. *Débutantes* are always rather heavy on hand, and you know, my Dearest, I want to shine as a hostess just because I am your wife."

Lencia thought that if the Ball ever took place, the number of young girls would be reduced to a minimum.

When they got out of the room, Alice said:

"She is determined to eclipse you, and I am not certain what we can do about it."

"There is nothing we can do," Lencia answered. "She dislikes us both and is determined we shall have as little attention as possible, not only from Papa, but from everyone else."

"I hate her," Alice said. "If she goes on like this, I shall go back to France and beg the *Duc* to take me into the Castle."

"Oh, Alice, do be careful!" Lencia warned her. "When you say things like that, I am always afraid someone is listening at the door and will tell Papa. Just think what a weapon against us the whole story would be in Stepmama's hands."

"That is true," Alice admitted. "Think what would happen to me. I would be locked in the Schoolroom here in the country. As it is, I doubt if I will be allowed to put a foot in Armeron House. She will be entertaining all the smart people who do not like young girls like us."

She spoke so bitterly that Lencia put her arms around her.

"Do not be unhappy, Darling," she said, "I feel that everything will come right in the end. I do not know how, but I just know."

"I hope you are right," Alice said. "Home is not like home anymore without . . . Mama."

Her voice broke on the last words.

Lencia could only hold her tight and kiss her.

"You will have to be brave," she said, "and we will fight this together. We must not let Stepmama get us down. That would be a victory for her."

"Yes, of course it would," Alice said, "and if Pierre were here, I know he would rescue me."

"I am sure he would," Lencia agreed. "But think of the commotion if he suddenly appeared saying what a lovely time we had in France."

Alice laughed.

"I would just like to see Stepmama's face! But she would be impressed with him because he is a *Vicomte*."

"Perhaps somehow when we go to London you can become acquainted with him. He did say he often comes here."

"I shall certainly try," Alice said, "and I promise you I will be very careful."

"You had better be, or Stepmama will shut us up here in the dungeon and we will never see daylight again."

They both laughed at this.

But when Lencia went to bed that night she was worrying about Alice.

She thought she must have a long talk with her Father.

She would suggest that if she was to be Presented at the last Drawing-Room, Alice should be too.

Lots of girls were Presented at seventeen, and Alice would actually be eighteen just before Christmas.

"Why did I not think of that before?" Lencia asked herself. "Then Alice can make some friends of her own age and go to parties which we hope will not include Stepmama."

She went to sleep thinking of Alice, and inevitably dreamt of the *Duc*.

The next day the Countess seemed to be determined to antagonise everyone she came in contact with, except, of course, the Earl.

She was very disagreeable to the Housekeeper about the condition of some of the rooms.

She told the cook the food had disgusted her because it was so English.

She informed the old Butler that the footmen were sloppy and a disgrace.

Lencia felt as if the whole house were vibrating against her.

'There was always a lovely atmosphere when Mama was here,' she thought. 'How can Stepmama upset everyone and everything so easily?'

Her Father wanted them to go riding with him.

The Countess, however, insisted he should take her driving round the Estate, as she had seen so little of it.

The girls went riding alone.

Because they were both somewhat depressed, they did not talk.

They jumped the low hedges and galloped over the flat ground.

When they got back to the Castle, Alice said:

"This is the first time in my life it has made me shudder to enter my own home. It used to be such a happy place."

"I know," Lencia said. "But I do not think Stepmama will stay here long. She will find it too dull. And when she and Papa go to London, perhaps we can have some friends to stay."

"Whom shall we ask?" Alice said. "Whom do we really want to be with?"

They both knew the answer to that.

Lencia never seemed to have a chance to talk to her Father alone.

However, the opportunity came after tea.

The Countess announced that she thought English tea was a waste of time, and perhaps they would like to dispense with it.

Both Lencia and Alice said quickly:

"No! Of course not."

To their relief, their Father said:

"I think that would be a great mistake. If there is one thing I dislike, it is breaking traditions which have been carried on for generations."

Their Stepmother acquiesced immediately.

"Of course, Dearest," she said, "you are quite right. It was very stupid of me to suggest such a thing. I was only thinking of saving the Servants. But that again was unnecessary, as you wisely, because you are clever, have pointed out."

She rose to her feet as she finished speaking.

She kissed the Earl on the cheek and said:

"I am going to lie down before dinner, because I hope to look beautiful and to entertain you by being witty."

"You are always that," the Earl said.

"But not as witty as you," his wife replied. "Someone in Sweden said to me that they had never known an Englishman as witty as you are."

The Earl looked pleased and the Countess moved towards the door.

"Do not be late for dinner, girls," she said severely. "You know how your Father hates to be kept waiting— bless his heart."

As she left the room Alice and Lencia looked at each other.

The Earl made himself more comfortable in his armchair.

"Now, Papa, we want to talk to you," Lencia said, "and make plans."

"Yes, of course," the Earl agreed. "We have not had a chance to talk about things until now."

Lencia sat down on one side of him while Alice sat on the hearth rug at his feet.

"This is like old times," the Earl said. "You know, my

Dearest, I love you both very much and want to do whatever will make you happy."

"I knew you would say that, Papa," Lencia said as she smiled.

"I must admit," the Earl went on, "I felt very guilty when I went to Sweden knowing how much Alice particularly wanted to see the Loire Castles. But I am sure it is something we can manage next year, if not before."

He sounded doubtful.

Lencia was certain that if he did suggest anything like that, their Stepmother would inevitably prevent it.

"Now, what I want to say to you, Papa is—" she began.

At that moment the door opened.

"Monsieur le Duc de Montrichard, M'Lord," the Butler announced.

chapter seven

FOR a moment everyone seemed frozen with surprise.

Then the Earl jumped up, saying:

"Valaire, my dear boy, I had no idea you were in London."

The Earl walked across the room to shake his hand, saying:

"I am delighted to see you, and it is far too long since you came here."

"I have come for your help," the *Duc* replied.

As he spoke, he saw Lencia for the first time.

As their eyes met, she put her finger quickly to her lips.

"My help?" the Earl repeated. "But of course, you know that I will help you in any way that I can."

He turned round, saying:

"Come and meet my family."

They walked towards Lencia and Alice.

They were standing, and feeling as if their hearts were beating too quickly for them to breathe.

"Now, this is Lencia," the Earl said as he reached her. "I think the last time you were ten years old and Lencia must have been only one, so you can hardly be expected to recognise each other."

"No, of course not," the *Duc* agreed, "it was a long time ago."

"And this is Alice," the Earl went on. "If she was born when you were last here with your Father, she would have been just in the cradle."

The *Duc* felt Alice press his fingers as if she was warning him.

The Earl went on:

"Now, can I offer you some refreshment? I suppose you have come down from London."

"No, thank you, I want nothing except to talk to you," the *Duc* replied.

"Where are you staying?" the Earl questioned.

There was a little pause.

Then with a smile which Lencia thought was irresistible, the *Duc* said:

"I was hoping for old time's sake that I might stay in Armeron Castle."

"But of course, my dear boy!" the Earl exclaimed. "Naturally we are delighted to have you."

"You must forgive me for not notifying you before I came," the *Duc* said, "but I made up my mind only at the last moment to come to England."

The Earl sat down in the chair he had been sitting in before, and the *Duc* sat next to him.

"Now tell me how I can help you."

Lencia held her breath.

She was aware that the *Duc* was thinking frantically what he should say.

"I seem to remember," he began slowly, "that your Father kept a diary, as did my Father. There is an author at the moment who is very eager to write his Biography. I wondered if in your Father's diary there would be any mention of the times my Father came here and what happened on those occasions."

"A Biography! What a splendid idea!" the Earl exclaimed. "And of course your Father was a very distinguished man. I have all my Father's diaries and they are in a special room upstairs. I will show them to you."

The Earl got to his feet and said to Lencia:

"You girls take the *Duc* to the Tower Room while I tell the Servants to arrange for his luggage to be taken upstairs and to notify your Stepmother that he is here."

"Yes, Papa," Lencia said meekly.

They all walked towards the door.

When they reached the hall, Lencia, the *Duc* and Alice went upstairs, leaving the Earl talking to the Butler.

Only when she was sure her Father would not notice, Lencia moved quicker.

They hurried down the passage to the room which contained relics of their Grandfather.

As they reached it, Lencia said to Alice in a whisper: "Keep cave."

She and the *Duc* went inside, and before she could speak he said:

"I have to see you alone, you realise that?"

"Yes, of course," Lencia answered. "But be very careful, Papa does not know we went to France."

"I guessed that when I saw your face, and you put your finger to your lips," the *Duc* said. "When can I talk to you?"

"When everyone has gone to bed," Lencia said in a low voice. "Go to the end of this passage, where you will find another staircase. At the bottom there is a door into the garden."

She ran across to the window and the *Duc* followed her.

"You see the fountain," she said. "If you look to the left of it, you will see there is a gate which leads into the Herb Garden. No-one will see us there. Papa's windows look out onto the other side."

She had hardly finished what she was saying when Alice said from the door:

"Papa is coming!"

Lencia turned towards the bookcase.

"Here are the diaries," she said, "and as you can see, there are a great number of them."

The Earl came into the room.

"It will take you some time, Valaire," he said, "to find what you are seeking. But if you were ten when you came here last, that is seventeen years ago, which will make it 1878."

"Of course, of course," the *Duc* agreed. "But my Father stayed with yours I think quite a number of times before that."

"He did, and we will just have to look and see what we can find," the Earl said.

Watching them, Lencia felt almost faint at the shock of seeing the *Duc* so unexpectedly.

At the same time, she was aware that her heart had turned a somersault.

It was difficult to think of anything except that he was there.

She could see him again and hear him after the hours she had lain awake thinking of him.

Only when they went to dress for dinner did Alice come into her room and say:

"I must know where Pierre is."

"We will find out before Valaire leaves," Lencia said, "but we must be very careful."

"I nearly gave a scream when he was announced," Alice said. "I thought I must be dreaming."

"I thought so too," Lencia replied.

At dinner she found it almost impossible to eat anything with the *Duc* sitting on the other side of the table talking to her Stepmother.

Or, rather, the Countess was talking to him.

She was absolutely delighted to have the *Duc* of Montrichard in the Castle.

She came down to dinner covered in jewels, and determined, Lencia knew, to make an impression on him.

"I have heard so much about you, *Monsieur*," she said in what she thought was her most fascinating voice. "My friends in Paris spoke of you so often."

She gave him a provocative glance from under her mascaraed eyelashes and went on:

"Of course they told me how many hearts you have broken and what a fantastic success you were."

"You must not believe all you hear," the *Duc* said.

"But I wanted to believe it!" the Countess said. "And I can assure you that you look exactly as I expected you to—so very handsome and *un vrai galant*."

She continued during the meal to flatter the *Duc* extravagantly.

It was the same way that she flattered her husband.

Listening, Lencia wondered if that was the sort of thing the *Duc* enjoyed.

If so, Lencia felt he could not really have enjoyed being with her in the way he said he had.

By the time dinner had finished she realised that she and Alice had said nothing throughout the meal.

She was sure that was exactly what her Stepmother intended.

When they moved into the Drawing-Room, the Countess sat beside the *Duc* on the sofa.

She continued to talk of Paris, and of the success he was with her friends.

"You may have a reputation," she said, "of being a very naughty boy, but who can blame you for that?"

"Who indeed?" the *Duc* replied.

He was looking towards Lencia as he spoke.

She found it an agony to hear her Stepmother talking on and on about his successes with other women.

She finally told her Father she was tired.

She and Alice slipped away without saying goodnight to their Stepmother or to the *Duc*.

"You see how she goes on," Alice said when they got outside the door. "If we had a Dinner Party for our friends, I do not suppose we should be able to say a word to them."

"Not if they were handsome and of any importance," Lencia said bitterly.

She went up to her room and stood waiting by the window.

It seemed that a Century passed before at last she saw the *Duc* walk across the lawn and past the fountain.

He found the gate she had told him about which led into the Herb Garden and disappeared inside.

It was then she hurriedly followed him.

Her Father and Stepmother's windows, as she had told him, looked out on the other side of the Castle.

There was no-one to see her run across the garden.

It was a bright moonlit night and stars filled the sky.

They glittered on the smaller fountain which was playing in the centre of the Herb Garden.

It made, she thought, an appropriate frame for the *Duc* who was standing with his back to it.

Now, having run across the lawn, she was moving more slowly.

When she reached him, for a moment it seemed as if both of them were stricken into a silence.

Then at last in a voice which did not sound like her own, Lencia asked:

"Why . . . did you . . . come . . . here?"

"How could you have gone away without telling me? How could you have left me in that cruel manner?" the *Duc* asked. "I was frantic when I thought I would never see you again."

"I . . . had to . . . go."

"Why?" the *Duc* demanded.

Because she did not want to answer that question, she said quickly:

"What made . . . you come . . . here of all . . . places?"

He smiled, and somehow it broke the tension a little.

"Alice left one of her books behind," he said. "It was, of course, about the Castles of the Loire, and inside was the book-plate of Armeron Castle."

Lencia gave a little exclamation.

"It belongs to the Library."

"That is what I thought," the *Duc* replied, "so I came to England at once to ask the Earl of Armeron if he had any knowledge of a Lady Winterton living in this neighbourhood."

"So that is how it happened," Lencia said.

"How could you have done anything so dangerous as to go alone with Alice to France?"

"When Papa, who had promised to take us, went instead to Sweden with our Stepmother," Lencia explained, "she was so disappointed. I did not . . . think it would be . . . dangerous if I . . . pretended to be . . . a married woman."

"Looking like you do, surely you must have realised there are men in France who would find you irresistible. Myself for instance."

Lencia said nothing, and after a moment he asked:

"Why did you go away so impetuously without saying goodbye?"

Still Lencia did not speak, and he went on:

"Were you not at all curious when I said I had something to discuss with you after I returned?"

"I knew . . . what that . . . would . . . be," Lencia said in a very low voice, "and . . . I was . . . afraid I . . . might say . . . yes."

The *Duc* stared at her for a moment, and then he said:

"What I was going to ask you, my Darling, was if you would do me the very great honour of becoming my wife?"

Lencia gave a gasp and looked up at him.

"You were . . . going to . . . ask me to . . . marry you?"

"As I am asking you now," the *Duc* said.

"But you . . . said after . . . what had . . . happened . . . you would . . . never marry . . . again."

"That was before I met you," he said.

He put out his hands and laid them on her shoulders, touching her for the first time.

"Now, listen to me," he said. "I knew from the very first moment I saw you not only that you were the most beautiful person I had ever seen, but also that in a way I could not explain, you belonged to me. Because of what

I went through as a young man, I had been determined to keep my freedom."

Lencia made a little movement, but he did not release her and went on:

"But when I saw you holding that baby in your arms, I knew I wanted you as my wife and the Mother of my children."

Lencia looked at him in surprise, and he said:

"But I was still fighting against what my heart and my soul told me, and that was why I came to your bedroom."

"Yet after . . . that, when I . . . sent you . . . away . . . you wanted to . . . marry me?" Lencia asked.

"I was always suspicious that you were not what you pretended to be," the *Duc* answered. "You seemed in many ways so young and so innocent and, although it seemed incredible—untouched."

Lencia blushed.

"You really . . . thought . . . that?" she asked.

"I thought it," the *Duc* replied. "Then, when I kissed you, I knew two things. First, you had never been kissed before, and secondly, you belonged to me completely and absolutely."

His voice deepened as he continued:

"I have never—and this is the truth, Lencia—felt so moved by a kiss which was different from anything I had ever known."

"Is . . . that . . . really . . . true?" she whispered.

"I think perhaps we should prove it," the *Duc* said.

He pulled her close against him and kissed her, at first very gently, and then more possessively.

It seemed to Lencia as if they were part of the fountain.

They were being thrown higher and higher up to the stars until they could touch them.

Only when the ecstasy which the *Duc* aroused in her seemed almost unbearable because it was so utterly and completely wonderful did he raise his head.

"Now you understand," he said in a deep voice. "Neither of us can fight against that. You are mine, Lencia, and I am yours, as God made us to be."

"I . . . love . . . you," Lencia whispered. "I love . . . you . . . I love . . . you . . . for what . . . seems to have been . . . a long . . . time. But I . . . never thought . . . you would . . . really love . . . me."

"I know exactly what you thought," the *Duc* said, "but, my Precious, neither of us can deny that what we are feeling now is so perfect, it can have come only from Heaven itself."

"That is . . . what I am . . . thinking," Lencia murmured.

"We think the same, we are the same, we are one person," the *Duc* said. "The question now is quite simple, how soon will you marry me?"

"As . . . soon as . . . you want . . . me to," Lencia said, and hid her face against his shoulder.

"That is now, this moment," the *Duc* answered. "But, my Precious one, I have something else to ask you, although you may think it a little strange."

Lencia raised her head.

"What is . . . it?" she enquired a little nervously.

"I want you to be very brave and run away with me," the *Duc* replied.

Lencia stared at him.

"Why?" she asked.

The *Duc*'s arms tightened for a moment, then he said:

"What we are feeling now is so perfect, so wonderful, I could not bear it to be spoilt."

"Nor . . . could . . . I," Lencia said.

"If we have a grand wedding such as everyone will expect," the *Duc* went on, "we shall have to wait for a month, perhaps more. During that time I know only too well that everyone will tell you stories about me."

He drew in his breath and continued:

"They may be true, but I do not want you to hear them. Even if you try not to listen, they will insist on talking of how many women there have been in my life, and a number of other things which I would much rather you did not know."

His voice strengthened as he said finally:

"They are past, they are finished with, they have no place in our future together."

Lencia knew exactly what he was saying.

She remembered how her Stepmother had kept referring to the love-affairs he had had in France with her various friends, and the way she called him "a naughty boy" and at the same time revelled in his naughtiness.

Lencia could understand how it would make everything seem rather cheap.

It would undoubtedly frighten her when she thought about the future.

The *Duc* was following her thoughts, and he said:

"Exactly! That is why, my Darling, I want you to be brave enough to come away with me immediately. Nothing and nobody must spoil the wonder and ecstasy we have found together."

His voice was very tender as he said:

"How you can make me feel like this I do not understand myself. I not only want you as I have never wanted a woman before, but it also makes me worship you because you are perfection itself."

"How can you say things like . . . that to . . . me?" Lencia asked. "At the . . . same time, it is what I . . .

want you to . . . feel if it . . . makes you happy."

"I am happier at this moment than I have ever been in my whole life," the *Duc* answered. "And I know now that when they called me *Monsieur Mille-Feuilles*, what I was seeking was a wife who loves me and a home where we will love our children together."

It flashed through Lencia's mind that he would be as kind and sweet to his children as he had been to the woodcutter's little boy, who had hurt his knee.

She moved a little closer to him and said in a whisper:

"I will . . . run away with . . . you, but you . . . must tell me . . . what to . . . do."

"My Precious, my Sweet, that is what I wanted you to say," the *Duc* exclaimed.

Then he was kissing her again, not only her lips, but her eyes, her little straight nose, and the softness of her neck.

It gave her strange feelings she had not known before.

"I have so much to teach you," he said as he felt her quiver. "And love, my Darling one, can be a very long lesson."

"I love . . . you . . . I love . . . you," Lencia said. "But how can we . . . run away without . . . everyone trying to . . . stop me?"

"That is exactly what they will do unless we are very clever about it," the *Duc* said.

He kissed her forehead before he said:

"When you left me, I was determined, if I ever did find you, that somehow I would take you away with me. Now it will be much easier than I thought it would be."

"But how! How!" Lencia asked.

"Today is Tuesday," the *Duc* said. "If I leave tomorrow, can you get to London on Thursday?"

"Yes, I can say I am going to ... the Dentist again," Lencia answered.

"Then I will collect you from Armeron House at eleven o'clock on Friday morning. We will be married, and then we will disappear until all the commotion and chatter about us has been forgotten."

"It sounds too ... wonderful," Lencia said, "but we will have to be ... very careful that ... no-one guesses what ... we are ... doing."

"You must be very careful," the *Duc* said. "Tell Alice, but no-one else."

With an effort, Lencia remembered that Alice wanted to know about Pierre, and she said a little tentatively:

"Where is ... Pierre?"

"He is in Hampshire, looking for Alice, where she told him she lived."

"And he wanted to find her?" Lencia enquired.

"He is very much in love with her," the *Duc* replied.

"How wonderful," Lencia exclaimed, "because Alice loves him! But how are we to get them together without Papa being suspicious?"

The *Duc* smiled.

"That is quite easy. Before I leave I will ask your Father if he would be kind enough to let my nephew see his horses. I know from what you told me he has some excellent ones. And if Pierre comes as a guest to the Castle, who would be surprised if they fall in love with each other at first sight?"

Lencia laughed.

"Oh, you are so clever! That is exactly what could happen without anyone thinking it strange."

"I will be honest with you," the *Duc* said, his eyes twinkling, "My sister and her husband were thinking of arranging a marriage for Pierre, and they would not have been prepared to accept Miss Alice Austin. Lady Alice Leigh of Armeron Castle is a very different matter."

Lencia laughed, and then she said:

"Please, Darling, arrange it. I want Alice to be happy, and she will never be happy living with our Stepmother."

"I thought that myself at dinner," the *Duc* said, "and that is another reason why I want you to come away with me as quickly as possible."

Lencia knew he did not want her to believe the stories her Stepmother would tell her about him.

Very stiffly she said:

"You know I think . . . you are . . . wonderful. Even if I have only two or three years of . . . perfect happiness with you, it will be . . . better than . . . a lifetime of . . . misery because I . . . refused you."

"I would not allow you to refuse me," the *Duc* said.

"And on our sixtieth Wedding Anniversary, or perhaps it will be our eightieth, you shall tell me what a wonderful husband I have been and you have never had a moment's worry about me."

Lencia laughed.

"Perhaps that is asking too much. But as long as you love me and as long as we are together, I shall feel as if I am living in Heaven."

Because she spoke so sincerely, the *Duc* could only kiss her until they were both breathless.

Then he said:

"I must send you to bed, my Darling. You have got a lot to do and to think about before Friday."

"I am . . . afraid," Lencia said, "I will not have a very elaborate trousseau."

The *Duc* smiled.

"I am a Frenchman, and I cannot imagine anything I shall enjoy more than dressing you as only a Frenchman can to make you even more beautiful than you are at the moment."

"I shall . . . enjoy that," Lencia murmured.

He kissed her again before he said:

"Go to bed, my Darling, and dream of me."

"That is what I have done ever since we left you," Lencia said. "Then, because I thought I would never see . . . you again, I have . . . cried."

"I will never allow you to cry in the future," the *Duc* said. "But if you cried, can you imagine how I felt when I had no idea where I could begin to look for you, except you had vaguely said you lived in Kent."

"Then they brought you the book," Lencia said. "It was very careless of Alice to leave it behind."

"It had slipped down the side of the bed," the *Duc* explained, "and I suppose because Alice was packing in a hurry she did not notice it was missing."

"But it brought you here, and how very grateful I am that Alice had a passion for seeing the Castles of the Loire."

"Now you will live in one and so will she," the *Duc* said. "God moves in a mysterious way, and we can thank Him on our knees that His way has been our way."

He kissed her again, and then he said:

"You are quite certain, my Precious one, that you do not mind being married secretly and with a rather short Service, as I am a Catholic and you are not."

There was a little pause, and then Lencia said:

"I have not thought about it for a long time, but actually I was Baptised a Catholic."

"How is that possible?" the *Duc* asked in astonishment.

"I expect my Father told your Father but you did not hear of it," Lencia said. "I was born in France. Papa was sent on a special mission to Paris when Mama was expecting me and had reached her seventh month. He wanted to go without her, but she said jokingly she would not trust him with all those beautiful French Ladies. Which I think now was very sensible of her."

The *Duc*'s eyes twisted because he knew she was thinking of his reputation.

He did not speak, and Lencia went on:

"While they were driving outside Paris they had a slight carriage accident. It was not a serious one, but Mama realised I had started to arrive too soon."

"What did your Father do?" the *Duc* asked.

"Papa took her into a Convent at St. Clois, where the Nuns looked after Mama and brought me into the world. Because I was so very small and they thought I might die, I was Baptised by their Priest."

She smiled and moved a little closer to the *Duc*, saying:

"I think I was born for you, so I lived. Of course, when we came back to England, I was Baptised again with the usual collection of Godfathers and Godmothers."

"But you were first Baptised a Catholic," the *Duc* said. "That makes things much easier."

"And, of course," Lencia said softly, "when we are . . . married I would like to . . . become a Catholic so that we can go . . . to Church together."

"With our children," the *Duc* added, "that is what I hoped and prayed you would say. As you must realise, my Precious one, that will make my home as perfect as I want it to be."

They moved across the Herb Garden.

When they reached the gate, the *Duc* kissed her passionately for a long time.

Then, as if everything were settled between them, they walked back to the Castle hand in hand.

Only when she was alone in her bed did Lencia say over and over again:

"Thank You, God . . . thank You for giving him to me."

*   *   *

The following morning the *Duc* left early.

Lencia began to sort out what clothes she would take with her to London.

She really had very few new dresses.

They were certainly not ones she thought good enough for her wedding.

There might not be anyone there, but she wanted to look beautiful for the *Duc*.

She wanted him always to remember their marriage, however quiet it might be.

When she told Alice what was happening, her sister was in a wild state of excitement, especially when she learned that she would see Pierre again.

"Do not look so excited at going to London," Lencia warned, "otherwise Stepmama may suspect something is up! The Dentist could not bring such a shine to your eyes."

"I love him, Lencia," Alice said, "and if he really loves me, could anything be more marvellous?"

The Earl suggested that he might go with them, but their Stepmother stopped that immediately.

She said she intended to be at Armeròn House the following week and the girls could then stay at the Castle.

She said she saw no point in everyone moving just before the weekend.

"I think it will have to be the week after that," the Earl replied, "because the *Duc* was telling me that his nephew, the *Vicomte* Béthune, is very eager to see my horses. I have suggested he come to stay this next Saturday for at least a week."

"The *Vicomte* Béthune?" the Countess said. "I should certainly like to meet him. I believe he is a very good-looking young man."

"All their family are," the Earl said in a lofty way. "And when he leaves, then, of course, my Dear, if you want to go to London, we will open the House."

"I will give several parties," the Countess said.

The Earl agreed.

But Lencia was aware that her Stepmother gave her a hard look as if to say she had no intention of including her in the parties.

'Fortunately,' Lencia thought, 'she does not know I shall be having the most perfect party of all on my own.'

She was well aware her Stepmother would be furious and intensely jealous when she learnt she had married a *Duc*.

She would also feel defrauded that she had not been able to have a grand wedding.

If she was not the Bride, she would at least have been the hostess!

"Valaire is right in thinking there is no need for all that," Lencia said to herself as she concentrated on her packing.

She took with her some very pretty night-gowns which had belonged to her Mother, also a lace-trimmed chiffon *négligée* which she hoped the Duc would find entrancing.

There was no point in including the gowns, except the one she had worn for dinner at his Castle.

They would make her look too old.

However, she had one plan that she thought was very important.

She and Alice travelled to London on the early train on Thursday morning.

They were accompanied by one of the older House-maids to look after them.

A carriage from Armeron House had been ordered to meet them at the Station.

When they stepped into it, Lencia told the footman she wished to drive to Bond Street.

She gave him the address of a shop where her Mother had always bought her clothes.

She had visited it with her several times.

When Lencia explained who she was, she was greeted warmly.

She said that she wanted a very beautiful white dress to wear for a special occasion.

The white afternoon-dresses were, however, she thought, rather unattractive.

They did not have the softness which she somehow felt was important.

A *Vendeuse* produced an evening-gown of white chiffon which was exactly what she wanted except for the bodice.

The woman, however, promised that by the evening she could fill in the neck and add sleeves to the gown.

This, Lencia knew, would make it a lovely wedding-dress for the *Duc* to see her wearing.

Because it clung to her figure and was a very soft material, she hoped it would remind him of the Goddess he thought her to be.

She also found two pretty day-dresses which suited her.

They were in pale colours which she hoped made her look like a flower.

She knew as they were being married secretly that she could not wear a veil or a Tiara at her wedding.

However, she found a hat which was a little more than a wreath of flowers.

It had just a surround of transparent material which made it somehow look like a halo.

"You look wonderful in that," Alice whispered, and Lencia hoped she was right.

They did not get to Armeron House until after tea-time, and the Servants were wondering what had happened to them.

"We had to go shopping," Lencia replied.

"We thought perhaps you'd had an accident, M'Lady," the Butler said

"No, I am quite safe," Lencia replied.

She and Alice had a quiet supper together and then went to bed.

It was impossible for Lencia to sleep because she was so excited.

At the same time, she knew that however angry her Father might be at the letter she had written to him, she was doing the right thing.

As Alice had said:

"Home is not home without Mama."

It would, in fact, Lencia thought, be far better for her Father if they were not there to irritate their Stepmother.

When morning came, the sun was shining.

Lencia got up early so as to allow plenty of time to make herself look beautiful for the *Duc*.

Alice came running upstairs to say he had arrived.

She went down feeling a little nervous because at that moment she was stepping out of her old world and into a new one, a world which she knew she had very little knowledge of.

But the *Duc* was the only thing that mattered.

He was looking extremely handsome, wearing what was correct in France, evening-dress.

His orders and decorations were on the breast of his evening-coat, while the ribbon of an order lay across his breast.

There was a diamond cross shining beneath his collar.

"You look magnificent!" Lencia exclaimed.

The *Duc* smiled and said:

"And you, my Darling, look exactly as I wanted you to look."

He kissed her hand and drew her outside to where there was a closed carriage waiting for them.

Behind it was one for Pierre and Alice.

The two young people did not say much to each other when they met.

But Lencia knew by the expression on their faces that they were very much in love.

This completed her happiness.

She would have been worried if she had left Alice alone and unhappy without her.

As they drove off in the carriage, the *Duc* said:

"This, my Precious, is the most exciting day of my life, and we are being married by Cardinal Vaughan, who is the head of the Catholic Church in England."

"Where are we being married?" Lencia enquired.

"In his private Chapel at the Archbishop's House in Westminster," the Duc answered.

"It sounds very grand," Lencia said.

"It is," the *Duc* replied. "The Cardinal has been very understanding, and when I asked for a Priest to marry us, he said he would do it himself."

The *Duc* gave a little laugh as he said:

"No-one can dispute after this that we are completely and properly man and wife, my Lovely one."

Lencia's fingers tightened on his.

"You are quite certain that you do not want to back out at the last moment?"

The *Duc* raised her hand and kissed it.

"I will answer that question better tonight," he said. "Now I am only thinking how much I love you, and how fortunate I am that I found you after such a long search."

She knew he was thinking of the flowers he had left by the roadside, and she said softly:

"I love you with . . . all my . . . heart and . . . my soul, it would be impossible to . . . love you . . . more."

"That is what you think now," the *Duc* said. "I promise you, my Precious, that our love will increase day by day and night by night."

They were married in a very beautiful Chapel which was filled with flowers.

The Cardinal was a tall, good-looking man and made every word he said seem as though it blessed them.

Pierre acted as Best Man and Alice was the other Witness.

There were two Servers and Incense Bearers in the Chapel but no-one else.

When they knelt and the Cardinal blessed them, Lencia felt the Angels were singing overheard.

She was sure a light enveloped them which could have come only from God.

Outside the Chapel the closed carriage was waiting and Lencia kissed Alice and Pierre goodbye.

As she drove off with the *Duc*, she asked:

"Where are we going?"

"My yacht is waiting at Westminster Bridge, which is a very short distance away," he answered.

They reached it in a few minutes.

Lencia saw it was a large and very impressive-looking yacht.

They were piped on board.

The Captain congratulated them and the *Duc* told him to move slowly down the Thames towards the sea.

There was luncheon waiting for them in a very attractive Saloon decorated in pale green.

"I never thought of 'our going away' in a yacht," Lencia said.

"What could be a better way to escape from the world than to be on the sea, where no-one can find us?" the *Duc* asked.

"And where are we going?" Lencia asked.

"To places you have never seen before and which I want to show you. Also," the *Duc* added quietly, "to a Heaven of our own."

Lencia smiled at him and took off her hat.

They ate the delightful food which she knew had been cooked by a French Chef.

It was impossible to think of anything but her husband sitting opposite her at the table.

He was looking at her with an expression in his eyes which told her without words how much he loved her.

When luncheon was finished and they were moving smoothly down River, the *Duc* said:

"Now we must follow French traditions which will be important to us in the future. There is one which is specially prevalent in France."

"What is it?" Lencia asked a little nervously.

"A *Siesta*, my Darling," he said. "That is what we both need and what we intend to have."

He took her below and into the master bedroom, which had of course been his.

It was filled with flowers which scented the air.

It was like a bower, and she said with an expression of joy:

"Have you really done this for me?"

"It is only one of the many things I want to do for you, my Precious," the *Duc* said. "But I hope you notice that the flowers are like you, white in their purity."

Lencia blushed, and he left her to take off his decorations.

She knew what he expected, and she undressed quickly.

She slipped into the large bed which was draped in the same way the bed at his Castle was draped.

In comparison, the cabin was small, but with all the flowers there was a fairy-like feeling about it.

It made Lencia think that everything that was happening was unreal and part of a dream.

"Suppose I wake up and find it is all untrue," she asked herself.

At that moment the *Duc* came into the cabin.

Impulsively she held out her arms.

"I was afraid . . . this might be . . . a dream," she said, "but . . . you are . . . here and I am not . . . dreaming."

"If you are, then I am dreaming too," the *Duc* said in a deep voice.

He sat down on the bed, looking at her.

"How can you be so beautiful?" he asked. "So perfect in every way and yet mine."

She put out her hand to touch his, feeling a little thrill as she did so.

"I am so . . . afraid," she whispered, "that I may . . . disappoint you."

"That is impossible," the *Duc* said. "You are everything I have looked for and thought I would never find. Now you are mine and nothing and no-one will ever take you from me."

"And you will . . . teach me . . . to . . . love you as you . . . want to be . . . loved," Lencia asked shyly.

"You can be quite certain of that," the *Duc* answered, "and it will be the most exciting thing I have ever done in my whole life."

He got into bed and took her into his arms.

As the shaft of sunshine she had felt before seemed to move through her, she knew this was the perfection of their love.

This was the moment when they would really belong to one another.

The *Duc* kissed her, at first gently, as if she were very precious.

She knew in a way the solemnity of the Marriage Service was still with him as it was with her.

Then his kisses became more possessive.

As his hand touched her, she felt the sunshine which was streaking through her body turn to fire.

She knew he felt the same as he kissed her and went on kissing her.

The flames seemed to rise higher and higher until the ecstasy of them made Lencia feel it was impossible not to die of its wonder.

Then, as the *Duc* made her his, they were both carried up in the sky.

They touched the sun and held the stars in their arms.

They were in the Heaven that God had made for lovers and which would be theirs for Eternity.

161

years by writing an average of twenty-three books a year. In the *Guinness Book of World Records* she is listed as the world's top-selling author.

Miss Cartland in 1987 sang an Album of Love Songs with the Royal Philharmonic Orchestra.

In private life Barbara Cartland, who is a Dame of the Order of St. John of Jerusalem and Chairman of the St. John Council in Hertfordshire, has fought for better conditions and salaries for Midwives and Nurses.

She championed the cause for the Elderly in 1956, invoking a Government Enquiry into the "Housing Condition of Old People."

In 1962 she had the Law of England changed so that Local Authorities had to provide camps for their own Gypsies. This has meant that since then thousands and thousands of Gypsy children have been able to go to School, which they had never been able to do in the past, as their caravans were moved every twenty-four hours by the Police.

There are now fifteen camps in Hertfordshire and Barbara Cartland has her own Romany Gypsy Camp called "Barbaraville" by the Gypsies.

Her designs "Decorating with Love" are being sold all over the U.S.A. and the National Home Fashions League made her, in 1981, "Woman of Achievement."

She is unique in that she was one and two in the Dalton list of Best Sellers, and one week had four books in the top twenty.

Barbara Cartland's book *Getting Older, Growing Younger* has been published in Great Britain and the U.S.A. and her fifth cookery book, *The Romance of Food*, is now being used by the House of Commons.

In 1984 she received at Kennedy Airport America's Bishop Wright Air Industry Award for her contribution to the development of aviation. In 1931 she and two R.A.F. Officers thought of, and carried, the first aeroplane-towed glider airmail.

During the War she was Chief Lady Welfare Officer in Bedfordshire, looking after 20,000 Servicemen and women. She thought of having a pool of Wedding Dresses at the War Office so a Service Bride could hire a gown for the day.

She bought 1,000 gowns without coupons for the A.T.S., the W.A.A.F.'s and the W.R.E.N.S. In 1945 Barbara Cartland received the Certificate of Merit from Eastern Command.

In 1964 Barbara Cartland founded the National Association for Health of which she is the President, as a front for all the Health Stores and for any product made as alternative medicine.

This is now a £65 million turnover a year, with one-third going in export.

In January 1968 she received *La Médeille de Vermeil de la Ville de Paris*. This is the highest award to be given in France by the City of Paris. She has sold 30 million books in France.

In March 1988 Barbara Cartland was asked by the Indian Government to open their Health Resort outside Delhi. This is almost the largest Health Resort in the world.

Barbara Cartland was received with great enthusiasm by her fans, who feted her at a reception in the City, and she received the gift of an embossed plate from the Government.

Barbara Cartland was made a Dame of the Order of the British Empire in the 1991 New Year's Honours List by Her Majesty, The Queen, for her contribution to Literature and also for her years of work for the community.

Dame Barbara has now written 611 books, the greatest number by a British author, passing the 564 books written by John Creasey.

AWARDS

1945   Received Certificate of Merit, Eastern Com-
       mand, for being Welfare Officer to 5,000
       troops in Bedfordshire.

1953   Made a Commander of the Order of St. John
       of Jerusalem. Invested by H.R.H. The Duke
       of Gloucester at Buckingham Palace.

1972   Invested as Dame of Grace of the Order of
       St. John in London by The Lord Prior, Lord
       Cacia.

1981   Received "Achiever of the Year" from the
       National Home Furnishing Association in
       Colorado Springs, U.S.A., for her designs for
       wallpaper and fabrics.

1984   Received Bishop Wright Air Industry Award
       at Kennedy Airport, for inventing the aero-
       plane-towed Glider.

1988   Received from Monsieur Chirac, The Prime
       Minister, The Gold Medal of the City of
       Paris, at the Hotel de la Ville, Paris, for
       selling 25 million books and giving a lot of
       employment.

1991   Invested as Dame of the Order of The British
       Empire, by H.M. The Queen at Buckingham
       Palace for her contribution to Literature.